NOOTKA

Vancouver Island

Tashees
Cooptee
Bligh I.

Friendly Cove
& Nootka Village

Nootka Sound

Pacific Ocean

NOOTKA

Being the Adventures
of John Jewitt, Seaman

MICHAEL HYDE

NEW YORK   HENRY Z. WALCK, INC.

Hyde, Michael
   Nootka; being the adventures of John
Jewitt, seaman. Walck, 1969
   184p. map

   Story, based on a true incident, of
the two survivors of a massacre aboard
the brig <u>Boston</u> in 1803.

1. Jewitt, John — Fiction 2. Vancouver
Island — History — Fiction 3. Indians
of North Ameri◯ca — Fiction I. Title

1513745

Contents

NOOTKA

Introduction

Boston has a splendid maritime history, and the "Boston Men" are an important part of it. They lived by and from the sea. Dr. Samuel Eliot Morison, in his book *The Maritime History of Massachusetts*, has written: "Maritime commerce was the breath of life for Massachusetts. When commerce languished, the Commonwealth fell sick."

Commerce did, in fact, languish, and the Commonwealth did fall sick in the years following the Revolutionary War. During the War itself, however, Massachusetts played a great part and prospered. Something like a thousand ships of her mercantile fleet were issued with Letters of Marque; that is to say, they became legalized pirates, or privateers, whose job was to prey on British commerce. At first, these ships made great profits from their privateering, but toward the end of the War, very many of them were captured by the British Navy; and in consequence the maritime life of Massachusetts suffered a setback. Her fishing, whaling, sea-trading and shipbuilding enterprises fell into decline and had to be built up anew. Her shipyards were building less than twenty ships a year, whereas before the War they were turning out more than a hundred.

But recovery came. And it came as a result of hard work and vigorous pioneering efforts; efforts to carry trade and the American flag into far-distant oceans and harbors—into the Pacific and Indian Oceans for instance; and into the China Seas, and the ports of Canton and Macao. Whalers began to round Cape Horn in pursuit of the whale. Boston brigs followed them, to compete in the Northwest fur trade. They left Boston in the fall, rounded the Horn at Christmas and arrived on "The Coast" in the spring. They carried cargoes of knives, copper plates, copper kettles, muskets, brass-hilted swords, soldiers' coats and buttons, pistols, tomahawks and blankets to trade with the Indians. What they wanted from the Indians (after treating them with ship's biscuit and molasses) were sea-otter skins to take to China where they could get very high prices for them. (Today, a sea-otter pelt could command a price of more than two thousand dollars.) And in exchange for their furs they took home from China to Boston good cargoes of tea and silk.

The Indians of "The Coast" spoke of the men aboard the Boston brigs as "Boston Men"; those aboard the English traders were "Kintshaushmen" (King George Men).

There appears to have been treachery on all sides. The traders sometimes treated the Indians unfairly; and the Indians were quick to take revenge, either upon the wrongdoers themselves or upon some innocent vessel. Occasionally whole crews were massacred. Up in the north, at New Archangel (Sitka), Russian traders were set upon by the Tlingit Indians. Farther south, off Vancouver Island, in 1811, John Jacob Astor's ship, the *Tonquin*, was boarded by Clayoquat Indians and the crew massacred. And earlier, at Nootka Sound, the men of the *Boston* were savagely done to death in 1803. Two only of the crew escaped with their lives, and they lived for almost three years as prisoners of the Indians.

John Jewitt, the young English blacksmith of the *Boston*, was one of the survivors; and he lived to tell the tale. He kept a journal in the ship's account book. When real ink ran out, he used wild berry juice, and for pens he used ravens' quills.

Rescued by another Boston brig, the *Lydia*, young Jewitt arrived eventually in New England where the *Boston*'s owners helped him to set himself up as a blacksmith in Middletown, Connecticut.

And it is recorded that there ". . . on the eighth day of March, in the thirty-ninth year of the Independence of the United States of America" John Jewitt handed in his Journal and Narrative to the Clerk of the District of Connecticut and had it registered "in conformity to an act of the Congress of the United States entitled 'An Act

5

for the encouragement of learning, by securing the copies of Maps, Charts, and Books, etc.' "

The story which follows is based on the true adventures of John Jewitt during his captivity at Nootka Sound.

I

Nootka: March 22, 1803

When I first came to my senses, I was aware of wood-smoke in my nostrils. Then, fearfully, I opened my eyes. I was lying in a dimly lit Indian longhouse. The embers of a hearthfire glowed on the ground. Above me the rafters were carved and painted; and through a gap in the flat roof a star shone with surprising brightness.

Then, suddenly, the star was gone, shut out by the head of an Indian leaning forward and looking down at me. It was the face of Maquinna, Chief of the Nootka Indians. At his side stood an Indian boy, gazing wonderingly at me in the dim light.

"Where am I?" I asked, fearfully.

My voice was meant to be loud and clear, but it sounded no more than a croaking whisper. My heart was thumping against my ribs. My ears were singing. My head throbbed violently; and my limbs were heavy and aching. The Indian Chief bent more closely over me.

"This—my—house, John," he said, in a low, slow voice.

"House," repeated the boy at his side.

I put my hand to my aching head. It was bound with large leaves around the temple. The leaves were wet and clammy.

"My head aches," I groaned.

"John's head hold much fire," said the Chief.

"Why is it so dark?" I murmured.

"John sleep long time," said Maquinna.

He turned his head to give an order to people round about in the darkness. Then someone stirred the embers, and a few flickering flames dispelled the heavy blackness all about. At the same time, other low fires began to blaze fitfully, and to light up the vast area of Maquinna's longhouse. A pleasant smell of woodsmoke wafted toward me.

Around the nearest fire, Indians were sitting on the ground. On one side were the men; on the other were the women, in blankets of colored bark cloth, their hair hanging in long braids. All were quite motionless. Painted or dyed blankets were hanging like tapestries on the outer walls. Others served as screens to divide this vast, barnlike place into living rooms. Large wooden chests and tub-shaped baskets stood about, by way of furniture.

While I was taking all this in, putting my hand to my aching head, and trying to moisten my parched lips with

8

my tongue, Maquinna gave another curt command to those nearby. At once, some of the women rose to their feet, and came to my side. One of them held a wooden bowl containing water while another filled and refilled a shell which she brought close to my mouth. I drank a great deal, and felt much better. My muddled senses began to revive. There was a tired, aching warmth in my limbs. I saw that my legs were covered by a greatcoat; and this greatcoat I recognized at once. It was Captain Salter's greatcoat, worn by him on the quarterdeck of the brig *Boston*.

Then it all came back to me in a sudden, terrible flood of remembering, and I was filled with horror and revulsion. With a cry, I sat up.

"You have murdered my shipmates," I gasped.

Maquinna leaned forward to calm me.

"Yes, John," he said. "No kill you, John. You live— work for me—make daggers."

"Daggers," repeated the Indian boy.

And so it was, that I, John Jewitt of Hull, England, the blacksmith and armorer aboard the *Boston*, came to be the captive of Nootka Indians. Why, as a lad, I went to sea; how I came to be captured; how I endured my captivity and contrived my escape; all this I will now set before you.

2

"I Want No Trouble with the Indians"

It was in the year 1802 that the brig *Boston*, out of Boston, Massachusetts, put into Hull, England, for repairs, and I went aboard her with my father to do the smith's work required for her tackle and rigging. When the work was finished, my father invited the Captain to our house in the High Street. My mother, I remember, made him a Capercaillie Pie to eat with his glass of ale.

I liked Captain Salter. He was a hearty man, rather red in the face, and portly. He told us about his voyages, and about trade with the Indians on the Northwest Pacific Coast of America. He told us about an Indian village at Friendly Cove, in Nootka Sound, Vancouver Island. It was Captain Cook who had called the place Friendly Cove, because he had found the people friendly—although Captain Salter said there had been troubles since. Captain Cook had given the Indians looking glasses, and they had given him valuable sea-otter furs in exchange.

"That's how the trade in sea-otter furs started," Captain Salter told us. "That's why we're making a trading voyage to the Northwest Pacific Coast. It's sea-otter skins we're after; and we're carrying a cargo of blankets, bar iron and muskets to trade for them."

Then I remember how the Captain looked steadily at me, before saying, in a loud voice, "You're a strong-looking lad, and I know you're skilled in your trade. How would you like to ship aboard the *Boston* as blacksmith and armorer, eh?"

Now I had read the *Voyages* of Captain Cook, sitting by the fireside on winter nights; and I had often, in my imagination, gone ashore with him, to meet the people of those far-distant shores.

"Oh, yes, sir," I said at once, "I should like to go with you very much."

The Captain smiled. Perhaps he had guessed that my heart was set on going to sea, anyway. Then he looked at my father. "What about it, Mr. Jewitt?" he said. "Thirty dollars a month; and he could make a bit extra, forging weapons on the passage out."

My mother, I remember, looked askance, while my father stroked his chin and pondered the matter; for it was his wish that I should follow him as a blacksmith in Hull, making harpoons and other gear for the Arctic whalers. But I was set upon going; and the long and the short of it was, that my father at length gave way. I was signed on as the *Boston*'s blacksmith, with permission to make copper daggers on the way out, to trade with the Indians.

From that day, until we set sail, I went many times aboard the *Boston* with my father, to fix up my forge amidships. The crew sometimes watched us at our work, giving us a friendly word or nod in passing. They were from many different countries, though about half of them were Americans, like Captain Salter himself and Mr. Ingraham, the second mate. Adam Siddle, the carpenter, was my fellow townsman. Jupiter Senegal was a Negro. The oldest and biggest man aboard was the sailmaker. Usually he was to be seen sitting amidships, in canvas trousers and rope shoes, his chest bare, and his hands busy with needle and palm, mending sails. He told me he had been born in Philadelphia; that he had run away to sea at the age of eight; that he had come to England as a cabin boy, and had been pressed into the Navy at the age of fourteen. His name was Thompson, but everybody called him Sails.

So the days passed. And then, on the second day of September, in my new sailor's hat and jacket, holding my sea chest on my shoulder with one hand and waving good-bye to my parents with the other, I went aboard.

We sailed out of Hull, southward to Cape Horn, and then northward through the Pacific Ocean until, six months later, on March 21, 1803, we were off Woody Point, at the entrance to Nootka Sound.

The Captain called us all on deck, trailing his eye slowly over us as we assembled. The sails flapped and bellied. Tackle chattered. The sea washed rhythmically at the ship's sides.

"Now, mark you well, men," the Captain began. "*I want no trouble with the Indians.* Make no mistake about that." Things had changed since the days of Captain Cook: there had been incidents—killings. And the Indians were now quicker to take offense, and to seek revenge.

"I shall go ashore in the longboat," said the Captain, "to pay my respects to Chief Maquinna, and to invite him aboard. They bring no weapons aboard; and we show none. Most Captains on the coast insist on that. So remember it, men. And remember that Maquinna can speak English, picked up over the years from the traders. Be careful to give no offense."

The sun was now low in the sky, shining brilliantly over the ocean to light up the distant cliffs. It fell golden on the craggy peaks of distant mountains, snow clad on the highest summits, and forested on the lower slopes. Woody Point and the entrance to Nootka Sound lay before us; soon we were sailing between pine-clad islands; and as the sun went down in splendor below the horizon, we saw above the trees a pale moon hanging in the darkening sky—a lantern to light us to Friendly Cove, and Indians.

3

Tyee Maquinna

Next morning, at dawn, the ship's bell roused the men below. They scrambled up on deck, stretching their limbs, blinking their eyes, and staring hard ashore to where the village of Nootka lay revealed.

A large clearing fronted the Sound, rising from a pebbly beach and backed and skirted by dense forest trees. On the beach, well clear of the water, a long line of canoes could be seen; and behind these were several wooden houses with carved posts shaped into human faces, beaked birds, and the fanged jaws of animals, vermilion red and blue and tawny yellow.

The houses were not particularly high, as houses go, but they were extremely long, with flat roofs. They lacked any window space, it seemed; but each longhouse had a huge carved and painted doorway. The largest of these longhouses, holding a commanding central position, was that of Tyee Maquinna, the Head Chief of Nootka.

As we gazed, the village came to life. Wisps of blue smoke began to rise. Soon, we saw people coming out from the dwellings. They looked at us, and then hurried toward us, down to the beach; men, women and children, making the dogs bark and the birds scatter above the headland of the Cove.

The Captain and a picked party of half a dozen men made ready to go ashore. They took with them one of my fowling pieces, intending to offer it, in goodwill, to Maquinna. We watched as the longboat pulled away with them, and took them across the still waters of the sunlit Cove. We shaded our eyes to see them the better, as they stepped ashore among the Indians and made their way slowly up the slope. A minute or two later they had entered Maquinna's longhouse, and were gone from sight.

On deck, the Mate sent us to our appointed tasks, until, after a surprisingly short interval of time, the cry went up that the shore party was coming aboard again. I ran to the ship's side, only just in time to see the Captain stepping on deck; and I saw, with some surprise, that he had brought the fowling piece back with him.

"Jewett!" he called to me, seeing me approaching.

"Aye, aye, Captain," I replied.

"Take a look at this fowling piece," he commanded. "What's wrong with it?"

He tossed it through the air toward me. I caught it

and, with some agitation, began to examine it. To me the gun appeared perfect in every particular. The crew gathered round, and watched in quiet curiosity.

"What's wrong with it, Jewitt?" demanded the Captain, curtly.

"Why, *nothing* is wrong with it, sir," I said.

"Exactly," replied the Captain. "Nothing is wrong with it. I don't know what's coming over these Indians. Maquinna says the lock is faulty."

I looked at the lock closely, and tested it again. "Why, no, sir," I said. "The lock works perfectly."

The Captain nodded his head. "Certainly it does," he said. "I tested it myself, and told the rascal as much, and with some heat. However, he's preparing to come aboard. So have another fowling piece ready, Jewitt."

"Yes, sir."

"And make doubly sure it's in good working order."

"I will, sir," I said, hurrying below.

I took another fowling piece from an arms chest, and made sure it was well oiled and in perfect working condition. Moreover, I chose one which had a little design inlaid in the stock, such as might take the fancy of an Indian Chief. I put it to one side, and went up on deck again, just in time to see some new activity on shore.

Tyee Maquinna was coming out of his longhouse, wearing a mantle of sea-otter furs. Six men followed him, walking toward the beach. A few moments more, and they had stepped into a splendid canoe. And now many other Indians began to run canoes into the water, and to man them, kneeling, their paddles hoisted in readiness to row.

On board, a sharp order from the Mate sent our men below and brought them back dressed for ceremony. Their varnished hats and the metal buttons of their jackets sparkled in the morning sunshine. The Captain gazed keenly at the scene. The Mate was beside him awaiting orders, and holding the Captain's speaking trumpet.

"Steward!" called the Captain. "Have some biscuit and molasses ready in the cabin." Then he turned to the Mate. "There's nothing they like better than a bit of treacle, these Indians," he said.

The steward moved off smartly to carry out the order, and the Captain turned to the Mate once more, to ask if all the ship's company were on deck.

"All save the sailmaker, sir. He was on night watch. Shall I bring him up?"

"No, Mr. Mate, let him be," said the Captain, after which he ordered the men to line the ship and give a welcome.

So a rousing cheer went up from the ship, startling the seabirds around the Cove, and frightening the fishes, for I saw a school that was swimming near the surface dive into deeper water and disappear.

Soon, it seemed, the shining morning sea was ruffled by a hundred and more paddles, as the canoes circled our ship, keeping at a distance of some fifty yards from us. And as they did so, the Indians gave voice to a plaintive chant, and every man kept time with his paddle. I recalled at that moment what I had read about Captain Cook's welcome to Friendly Cove: this, I thought, was how the great navigator had been received by these very men, though many of them must have been but boys at the time.

As each canoe rounded the stern of the ship, the Indians rose up and gave a great shout. This continued for some time, and then Maquinna's canoe broke from the ring of circling boats to come alongside us.

At that moment, I saw the Mate turn uneasily to the Captain. "How many will you allow aboard, sir?" he asked.

"Maquinna and his boat's party, that's all," said the Captain. "It's the usual procedure. I shall take Maquinna into my cabin and talk trade. You will look after his party on deck, if you please. Show 'em the ship: that's what they like. But don't encourage them to handle things too much. A bit light-fingered, some of them."

Maquinna's canoe came alongside, and his party climbed aboard with bundles of sea-otter furs. Last of all, the Chief himself came on deck, and the Captain stepped forward to greet him.

"Welcome aboard, Tyee Maquinna," said the Captain.

The Indian Chief stood for a moment, unmoving. All eyes were upon him. He was tall and straight, dignified and well-proportioned, with a fine nose, and a face and arms of a dark copper hue. His shiny black hair was powdered with white down, and circled by a colored headband. His magnificent black cloak of sea-otter furs was held around his body by a broad, ornamental belt. He moved forward a step to the Captain. Two of Maquinna's men now ran forward, and placed a number of furs at the Captain's feet.

"You are a great Chief, Tyee Maquinna," said the Captain. "These are fine sea-otter furs. I thank you for them. Let me offer you some ship's biscuits and molasses. Be good enough to step into the cabin."

Maquinna went in, followed by the Captain, and very soon I was called to join them. I stepped inside, and stood waiting to be noticed, just inside the door.

"Step forward, Jewitt," said the Captain. "This is my blacksmith and armorer, Tyee Maquinna. He looks after all the arms."

Maquinna looked me up and down as though I were for sale. Then he turned to the Captain. "He—is—young," he said.

"Yes," replied the Captain. "But he knows his job, and I'm very pleased with him."

"What—your—name?"

"John Jewitt, sir."

"John . . ." said Maquinna in his deep voice, so that it sounded like a gong. "You—make—daggers?"

"Yes, he can make daggers," put in the Captain. "He's made a quantity on the voyage out. You saw his forge, maybe, amidships. What else have you made, Jewitt? Tell Tyee Maquinna what you've made."

"Bracelets, sir, and copper bangles, and beads."

"Good," said Maquinna. "It is good."

"Well, now, Jewitt," said the Captain, breezily, "we'll make Tyee Maquinna a handsome gift. Bring the best-looking fowling piece you can find, Jewitt. Test the lock, and make quite certain it's in good trim."

"Yes, sir; very good, sir."

I turned smartly, and ran below to get the fowling piece. On my way, I noticed, through a porthole, some Indian canoes very close to the ship; but I was so engrossed with the importance of my errand that I gave no further thought to this. A few moments later, I had picked up Maquinna's gun, and was giving it a final inspection, so as to be sure there would not be one single speck of dust on it. Suddenly, up on deck above me, I heard the most horrifying tumult, with shrieks and cries so bloodcurdling that even now my dreams are haunted by it.

The next moment, I found myself leaping for the companion stairs, obeying some instinct to get away. I remember seeing the patch of sky above; then the dark face of an Indian filling the gap, the flashing of a tomahawk, and a hand clutching at my pig-tailed hair; and I fell backwards with a cry of terror—backwards down the companion steps, stunned and senseless.

4

Tom-soon

I do not know what happened immediately after my fall down the companion steps. All I can remember is that I opened my eyes to find myself in Tyee Maquinna's long-house, with the Chief himself at my side, and a bright star twinkling through a gap in the roof boards. I remember too that owls were hooting outside, in the night air.

"Why did you kill my shipmates?" I found myself whispering to him in a thin, hoarse voice. It was a question which haunted me continuously in the following days. Vaguely, I recalled how Captain Salter had said on different occasions that the old friendship between Indians and white traders was being much strained. There had been faults on both sides.

I recalled the mysterious incident of the fowling piece. Maquinna had complained about a faulty lock; and Captain Salter had perhaps flared up in anger at this. Had a quarrel been deliberately picked? I had read that Indians always revenged an insult . . . but surely—surely not by wholesale massacre?

"Why did you kill my shipmates?" I said again.

Maquinna did not reply for some time. Then, calling for quietness all around, he lowered his head toward me, and spoke word by word, very slowly.

"John—I tell you," he said. "Between white man and red man—much trouble."

"Trouble?" I repeated. "What trouble? What do you mean?" He motioned to me to be silent and to listen to his words. I nodded my head to show that I understood. Then, with an occasional movement of head or hand to give weight to his words, he told me of the troubles that had come to his land since he first gave sea-otter furs to Captain Cook.

"Captain Cook—good man," he said, and went on to tell of the coming of the great navigator to Nootka, in the days when all was well. Another Indian chief, Wic-an-an-ish, was staying with Maquinna on a friendly visit when the *Resolution* put into Nootka Sound. Captain Cook had given both of them presents. Those times were good times. How different from now. . . .

And then he told me this.

Only a little while before our arrival, it seemed, another white trader had put into Friendly Cove, while Maquinna was away, visiting Wic-an-an-ish. In his absence, the crew had come ashore, had entered Maquinna's house, and had stolen many of his furs, shooting the men who tried to stop them and frightening the women and children.

And it slowly dawned on me that Maquinna had wreaked vengeance on us for the wrongdoing of another ship's crew. I groaned. The Captain's voice was in my head, saying, "Mark you well, men: *I want no trouble with the Indians.*"

Maquinna could see how exhausted I was. He spoke no more. The inhabitants of the longhouse stirred the hearthfires, and began to move to and fro. I closed my eyes and tried to go to sleep. But I could not rest. My tired eyes were striving to penetrate the dimness all about.

There were no windows in the great house; only movable planks on the roof to let the smoke out and the starlight in. I gazed upward at the star through the chink in the roof; and I wondered if perhaps that same star had sometimes shone on me through the attic window of my bedroom at home in England.

Then I began to think of my mother and father; of the smithy behind the house, where we made harpoons for the Arctic whalers; and of the wharves at the waterside where I had lingered so long, watching the ships. I recalled my first sight of the *Boston* as she came into Hull for repairs. I remembered Thompson, the old sailmaker, and how he used to sit amidships, near my forge, sewing sailcloth. I thought of Jupiter Senegal, too, one of the Negroes aboard, who had always shown me such a friendly smile. And I thought of the ship's carpenter,

Adam Siddle, my fellow townsman; and of Mr. Ingraham, the second mate, who had drawn such fine pictures
of albatrosses seen on our voyage . . . And I thought
again of those Saturday evening songs during the dog-
watches.

And then, as I touched the Captain's greatcoat, now
spread over me as a blanket, I shuddered, and thought of
Captain Salter and of all the rest of my murdered shipmates. The words of the Captain kept running in my
head and would not leave me: "*I want no trouble with
the Indians. . . .*"

At last, I drowsed off into a fitful sleep, so that I do not
know how much later it was that I was startled by a sudden commotion in the longhouse. With a cry, an Indian
ran in from outside. He was shaking as if with fear.
There was a rapid exchange of words and gestures, as the
other Indians gathered around him; and a moment later
they had all turned to direct fierce glances at me. They
began to move toward me; but Maquinna held them
back.

"John—my man come from ship," he said. "My man
see white man 'board ship."

My heart began to race. For a while I was unable to
speak for lack of breath. Then, at last, the words came
from me. "A white man!" I exclaimed. "Alive, you
mean?"

Maquinna nodded. "White man strong. Him big man.
Knock my man down."

"Tyee Maquinna," I pleaded, "please let me go to him. Let me see my shipmate."

"Yes, John. You go 'board ship. Bring white man."

"You will not kill him, Tyee Maquinna?"

Maquinna's face was hard and expressionless when he answered. "White man use fist. Knock my man down. Him kill. John bring white man ashore. Come."

Maquinna put his sea-otter mantle about him, picked up a club from beside his sleeping couch, brushed the other Indians aside, and bade me follow him. And in my heart was dark terror.

Several of the Indians came after us, carrying burning torches. We went out into the night, toward the beach. An owl hooted in the trees behind us, the sea plashed gently on the pebbles, and a pale moon, low in the sky, revealed the ship, riding forlornly at anchor.

"John—you go 'board. Bring white man 'shore," ordered Maquinna.

Two Indians ran a small canoe into the water for me. I stepped into it, grasped a paddle, found my balance, and skimmed out over the water. I reached the ship and climbed aboard in the darkness.

All was silent and still on the ship's deck. Some of her timbers groaned a little, and water lapped gently at her sides; but these sounds, in the stillness of the night, served only to accentuate her deathlike calm. And there I stood, hardly daring to move. Somewhere, hidden, was my shipmate.

As I stood there, my eyes became more accustomed to my surroundings. I could make out a seaman's stocking cap caught in the shrouds, swaying ever so slightly in a breath of moving air. It was hanging limply there, as if it had fallen from the head of its owner, perhaps as he tried vainly to escape into the rigging. Close to the cabin I could distinguish a dark stain. I shuddered, half expecting to see bodies of my murdered shipmates propped against ship's tackle perhaps, or in the scuppers. Yet clearly their bodies had all been thrown overboard to the rocks and the seaweed ten fathoms under. It was too horrible to think of; yet I could think of nothing else.

I moved stealthily forward to the top of the companion, and there I halted again. The thought crossed my mind that my shipmate, in the darkness, might mistake me for an Indian.

At last I took heart, and in a voice that I tried to make bold, called out, "Where are you?"

The sound of my own voice startled me. It was as though I had stirred up a score of ghosts. I held my breath, clutched the companion rail, and listened. All I could hear was the racing of my heart, thudding against my ribs. I had no courage to shout again, but moved slowly down the companion stair into the heavy darkness below, whispering as I went, "Where are you? Where are you?"

Then, at last, out of the blackness came a voice; and there was no mistaking whose voice it was. It was the gruff, strong voice of the sailmaker, Thompson, who had been down below deck at the time of the massacre.

"It's the blacksmith. Young Jewitt . . ."

His face came close to mine, so that I could see the whites of his eyes, and feel his breath, smelling of tobacco.

"There's blood on your face, lad. The murdering heathens . . . They're not using you as a decoy, lad, are they? Are you alone? Who's behind you?"

"Nobody, Sails," I whispered. "I'm alone. Maquinna sent me to bring you ashore."

There was a tremor in my voice. But this was not echoed in the voice of Thompson.

"He's going to kill me, is he? Not without a struggle, he ain't."

"Listen, Sails," I said. "I'll tell you what I'll do. I'll tell Maquinna you are my father."

I suppose it was the dire extremity of the situation that put this notion into my head. I was clutching at a straw. But the effect it had on Thompson was quite unexpected. He gave a heavy, rumbling sigh.

"The poor lad's lost his reason," he mumbled. "And little wonder: he's been struck on the head, and they've tied it up with leaves, the murdering heathens."

"Listen to me, Sails. And try to understand."

"I'm not afeared to die," he cut in.

"There's no need to die, if you will pretend you are my father."

27

At length, I persuaded the fiery old man to follow me, and I fumbled my way to the deck. All the time, he was cursing the Indians for murderers and heathens, and vowing vengeance on them. As we reached the deck, and saw the dusky figures of our captors in a pool of torch-light on the beach, he exploded with eagerness to be at them. "Let's turn the cannon on 'em!" he begged; and when I refused to listen, he turned on me, called me a coward, and cursed me as roundly as he had been cursing the Indians a moment before. But by dint of hard plead-ing and even harder swallowing of insults, at least I per-suaded him that the best thing for both of us was to submit. It was our only chance of survival. He lowered himself heavily into the canoe, almost overturning it; and I paddled him to the shore, and led him before Maquinna.

The information that Sails was "my father" tumbled from my lips. I repeated it several times, each time more urgently than the last. As I did so, Maquinna was eyeing me very strangely, I thought. Then he turned his atten-tion to Thompson. My shipmate was breathing heavily. Out of the corner of my eye, as we stood there side by side, I could tell that his fists were clenched. For a mo-ment or two which seemed endless, there was silence. Then Maquinna spoke at last, pointing at Sails as he did so: "John—tell me his name."

I was nervously straining to form words to say that his name was Jewitt—since, if he were my father, that must surely be his name—when my fierce old shipmate shouted out in defiance, "Me name's Thompson!"

I caught my breath at this blunder. Why must the old man be so obstinate? I just stood there, trembling, waiting for Maquinna to order his men to fall on us. But he seemed in no hurry to do so. Indeed, the name of Thompson seemed to be having a strange effect on him, as though expressing a kind of magic. "Tom-soon," he murmured. He was relishing the name. Perhaps it resembled some Indian word of great portent—a word of hope or good fortune; or the name, perhaps, of some Indian spirit or god.

"Tom-soon," said Maquinna. "Tom-soon—that is good. Tom-soon live in my house. Work for me. John—Tom-soon—come."

5

Return to the Brig

We followed Maquinna into his dimly lit longhouse. Thompson was silent and sullen, though my own relief was unbounded.

Some of the Indians gathered inquisitively near us. Others peered at us from a distance. Maquinna pointed out a bench next to mine, on which Tom-soon could lie for a bed. He lay on it without a word, folding his arms across his chest, and staring through the roof planks at the stars. Silently, Maquinna and the onlooking Indians moved away, although they remained within the longhouse.

Soon, I noticed that my shipmate's eyes were closed; before long, his breathing became regular and peaceful, and a little while later he actually began to snore. Anyone would have thought him the most contented of men, at peace with all the world.

I cannot say how glad I was to have him by my side. Though I could not sleep myself, his deep snores comforted me, allayed my terrors, and gave me heart to face whatever the dawn might bring.

I must have fallen asleep at last, because I opened my eyes to see daylight streaming in through the gaps in the roof and through fissures in the side of the great cedar-plank house. Sails was still fast asleep, breathing heavily beside me. I rubbed my eyes, sat up, and blinked at the bright shafts and beams of light crisscrossing the vast and shadowy interior. Then, to my amazement, I became aware that Sails and I were alone in the house.

I rose stiffly from my couch of cedar planks to wake my shipmate. Then I thought better of it, and instead moved toward the door. As I left the dark house, and came out into the dazzling sunlight, I heard the sound of many excited voices. I saw the Indians down on the beach, and out on the water of the Cove. Some canoes were already tied up alongside our ship, and men were swarming all over her.

I sat down upon the ground, feeling very woebegone. Indeed, such a feeling of faintness and distress came over me that I dropped my head in my hands and sobbed. And while I was in this unhappy frame of mind, I felt a hand suddenly grip my shoulder and, glancing quickly up, I saw the large unshaven face of my shipmate looking down at me.

"Never mind, lad," he said. "Never mind. We'll stick together and see it through." He handed me some ship's

31

biscuit from one of his pockets. I was glad to eat it, and felt better for it.

He sat beside me, and stared hard toward the poor old *Boston*, at anchor in the Cove; and I could see his eyes were smoldering, and his mouth was set.

As we sat, beholding the dismal scene, I told him why Maquinna had massacred our shipmates; for now it seemed that he was taking our ship as a handsome recompense for the furs so recently stolen from him by the men of another crew.

Meanwhile, Maquinna came toward us from the beach.

"John—Tom-soon—you come," he called. "You come 'board ship."

We went down to the large canoe that his men held ready in the water. Maquinna took up a position amidships and motioned us to do the same. Then, at a word, his men jumped in, and knelt fore and aft of us, using their paddles in unison with fine and graceful sweeps. Maquinna's canoe cannot have been less than fifty feet in length, beautifully shaped and trimmed; and for all her size, she sat upon the water like a sleek bird, and skimmed over it with effortless ease toward the *Boston*.

Many of the Indians were now aboard the ship. They had thrown off most of their clothes, and were climbing the rigging, leaping from one yard to another with the agility of acrobats. Others were hanging from her sides, or dropping and diving through her ports into the sea, shouting and laughing like children at a new game.

We climbed aboard. The first thing I saw was my forge amidships, at which I had spent so much time on the way out. The iron bars, sheet metal, and copper nails had disappeared. Two Indian youths were dipping their hands in the coal box and smearing black streaks over their bodies.

Maquinna moved toward them in anger, and the two culprits dodged quickly aside. Then, Maquinna shouted an order which brought everyone down from the rigging, or up from below deck; and the unloading of the ship began in earnest. For Thompson and myself, it was a sad sight indeed.

"Sails, what about our sea chests?" I said, in sudden despair, for a seaman without his sea chest is lost.

"Aye, lad—the sea chests! We'd best get 'em before it's too late."

"We ought to take the ship's papers too," I said, and he agreed. "Lad—that's the first thing the owners are going to ask when we escape. 'Where's the ship's papers? Did you get the ship's papers? Why not?' That's what they'll say."

"They'll be in the Captain's writing desk," I said.

I went up to Maquinna, and asked for permission to take our belongings ashore.

"You take, John. You take," he said, without hesitation.

The Captain's desk was locked, but the key lay beside it. Inside, we found the ship's papers and a blank account book. Also in the cabin, I found a Bible, a Book of Common Prayer, and the *Voyages* of Captains Cook, Meares and Vancouver. All these I put into the Captain's writing desk, or into my sea chest, which I had now taken into my possession. Meanwhile Sails was gathering up some small tools belonging to the ship—knives, chisels, bradawls and the like—to put into his own chest.

"Sails, have you seen the *Nautical Almanack?*" I asked. We began to look for it. The *Almanack* would be very useful to us in a number of ways. It was full of valuable information, including, of course, the calendar. Sails searched among the cabin furniture. Then, after a darting look out on deck, he suddenly shouted, "Ah—there it is, lad. Get it from him quick!"

I looked out, just in time to see an Indian holding the *Almanack* carelessly by a few opened leaves. He looked as though at any moment he might throw it into the sea. But in a matter of seconds, Sails had reached him, grabbed him by the arm, and taken the *Almanack* from his grasp. Shocked by this rough treatment, the Indian looked very displeased. Quickly, therefore, I took from my sea chest one of the copper bracelets which I had made on the voyage out, and ran to offer it to him. His expression changed in a moment to one of forgiveness. And the *Almanack* was ours.

We lowered our sea chests and the Captain's writing desk into Maquinna's canoe and sat on them until we reached the shore. We carried them between us to our appointed places in Maquinna's house, where we left them, securely locked. The keys we kept on strings around our necks. I also carried in the same way a horse-shoe clasp that my mother gave me when I left home. So far, it had brought me little good luck, I thought.

All that day, and all the next, the Indians were carrying cargo ashore. They took the ship's longboat, and beached it near the canoes. And then, in the evening, over a meal of salmon and whale oil, Maquinna spoke to us.

"John," he said, "tomorrow, you go 'board ship. Make me fine dagger. Tom-soon go 'board ship 'long you. Him make me one big sail—fix my canoe. Many people come —many canoes. I give them many things. It is good for me to give many things. I show them dagger made by John. I sail my canoe with big canvas made by Tom-soon."

It was the custom of these Indians, it seemed, to hold ceremonies to which they invited neighboring tribes. At these ceremonies, they gave away many gifts, because, according to their custom, the more gifts they could give away, the more advantage they could gain over the other Indians. To receive gifts was not so good as to give them. *"One who receives many gifts becomes a slave."*

So Maquinna was planning to give away to other tribes much of the *Boston*'s cargo. In so doing, he intended to hold the position of the most powerful Chief on the Coast, because he could give away in gifts more than anybody else.

While we were eating our supper—without, I must say, much enjoyment—Maquinna's son, Sat-sat-sok-sis,

35

stood beside me. All day he had looked long and covet-ously at the silver buttons on my jacket.

"Buttons," I said.

"But-tons," he repeated.

"You—like—buttons?" I asked.

"Like but-tons, yes; yes, yes," he replied, eagerly.

Whereupon, I pulled off my silver buttons, threaded them on a string, and hung them around the boy's neck. He was delighted. He jumped for joy. And from that time forth he regarded himself as my inseparable friend.

As for Maquinna, it was as if I had indulged in my very own Gift-giving ceremony, with the purpose of im-proving my own social standing. There was no doubt that I had gained in his esteem.

"Tomorrow, you go 'board ship," he repeated. "John make dagger. Tom-soon make one big sail—fix my canoe."

6

Ships Ahoy!

The next day, Sails and I were up with the dawn, and rowing ourselves out in the ship's longboat to the now deserted *Boston*.

"Look, Sails," I said, with some excitement, pointing to seaward. About half a mile away there was a run of whales, spouting. The fine spray glistened in the sharp sunlight. Indians along the cliff, on the far side of the Cove, had seen them too. But my shipmate was in an ill mood. *He* didn't want to see whales. All he wanted to see was a ship coming in to rescue us.

"You can tell me when you see a brig bearing down," he growled. "And until then you can hold your peace, and let me hold mine."

"Sorry, Sails," I said, feeling the rebuff.

But the Indians, Maquinna included, and Sat-sat his

son, were also excited by the whales in the offing. I had already learned that the Nootka Indians were skillful whalers. They went far out to sea after whales and caught them with spears and harpoons tipped with mussel shells.

We reached the ship, and Sails climbed aboard. For myself, I decided first to bathe in the cool, clear water of the Cove. The sun was shining on the water; the sky was pale blue with a few fleecy clouds, and the sweet smell of the pine and spruce forest wafted across on the offshore breeze.

I swam around in the water, kicking and splashing about, and enjoying myself. I dived under the surface into the cool, clear water. There were rocks down below that I could clearly see. And then, either I saw, or I thought I saw, something that made me shudder; made me rise to the surface quickly; made me climb into the boat and drag the clothes over my wet, dripping body. For what I saw, or thought I saw, was the massacred body of Jupiter Senegal, the Negro cook, lying deep down there, among the rocks, in a watery shaft of sunshine.

I climbed quickly aboard. Sails was already at work. He was sitting with bolts of sailcloth about him, busy with his cutting knife, needle, and sailmaker's palm. He looked at me rather sourly.

"Sails . . ." I began. Then I thought better of it, and held my peace. What use to tell him what I had seen, except to make him curse our captors all the louder, and our own misfortune more continuously?

I took a look around the ship. It was a woebegone sight, to be sure. The sails were cut away from the yards, hanging by a corner and flapping against the rigging; or lying untidily in heaps on the deck. It was no surprise to me that Sails kept his eye down on his work, and suffered our humiliation in angry silence.

I went below decks. The arms chests and powder magazines had been broken open. There was litter everywhere: bits of metal strewn about, buttons lying in the scuppers, sailors' stocking hats caught on the windlass, pages from books, a few stray coins, packets of tea, pieces of salt beef and pork left unwanted, bars of soap, and even boxes of chocolate.

I picked up a box, intending to make a breakfast of chocolate, and went on deck. It was a relief to breathe the fresh sea air again. I went up to my shipmate.

"Sails," I said, thinking to cheer him, "they haven't taken off any of the salt beef and pork. There's enough to last us for months, if not years." He withered me with a look.

"Lad," he said, sourly, "don't talk to me about months and years. Don't talk to me." He spat, and continued with his work on the little square sail for Maquinna's canoe. He declined, with a shake of his head, the chocolate I offered him. I went to my forge; but I hadn't the heart for work. And my sea chest contained many daggers already made and concealed beneath layers of my clothes. One or two of these I could give to Maquinna.

I looked out to sea, and on both sides, around the Cove. Whales were still surfacing, blowing and diving, not far off. The Indians were still watching them from the cliff. Maquinna was there, using Captain Salter's spyglass. Sat-sat was at his side, and evidently pestering his father for a turn because I saw Maquinna eventually pass the spyglass to his son, pointing in the direction where he must look. It was a wonderfully clear day.

Next, I saw a party of Indians on the beach, running Maquinna's canoe into the water. They seemed to have equipped the canoe with lines and spears and harpoons. The men jumped in, fell upon their knees, and instantly paddled the canoe into deeper water, until they reached the beach below the cliff on which Maquinna was standing. Maquinna left Sat-sat, descended the cliff and got into the canoe. Once aboard, the canoe slid swiftly out of the Cove toward the open sea. I watched it go, never taking my eyes off it. I saw it slacken speed, and then stay still. The men shipped their paddles. The water all around the canoe was sparkling like diamonds.

Suddenly I saw Maquinna stand upright in the bow of the canoe. I saw the harpoon, like a dart of light, leave his hand. Then the men in the canoe were clearly hanging onto the sides of the canoe with both hands, as the line ran out, and the whale, fast on the harpoon, was taking them for a ride. And in a moment, they were out of sight, behind an island where seabirds flew.

It then occurred to me that, by climbing the rigging, I could keep the whale hunt in view. Therefore I leaped upon the shrouds and ran up the ratlines, hand over hand, until I reached the topmost yard. I sat astride the yard, keeping a sure grip. I was breathless. The breeze ruffled my hair. I was level with the tops of the nearest trees ashore, and with the roof of Maquinna's house. Sails, down on the deck, seemed a long way below.

My attention, at that moment, was drawn to the Indians on the nearby cliffs. They were becoming very excited, and I searched the coastline, as best I could, against the bright sun, for the cause of this commotion. But I could see no sign of Maquinna's canoe. The whale, I thought, had drawn it to some part of the sea now obscured by the promontory.

And yet the Indians were becoming more and more excited, pointing out to sea and making a great noise. They seemed to be looking, however, in the direction almost opposite to the one the canoe had taken, and farther out to sea. And then, as I turned my head to look, my heart almost leaped into my throat, and what I saw caused me, for a moment, to lose my grip, so that I was in danger of hurtling to the deck below.

Out in the Sound, and still quite a long way off, were two ships. One had yellow sides and a figurehead. The other, with red sides, resembled a French corvette.

For a moment or two, I could do no more than gaze stupidly at them, coming in under full sail. It seemed as if I were dreaming, or seeing a mirage. Then I got my voice.

"Sails!" I shouted down to him. "Two ships. Coming in fast!"

He knew better than to think I was playing a joke on him. He was on his feet at once; the sailcloth on which he was working was flung aside; and he was climbing the shrouds like a man half his years. Almost at once he was just below me, and had seen the ships. Then he became well-nigh frenzied.

"Shout, lad—burst your lungs—shout! Ahoy! Ahoy! Wave, lad. Wave and shout!"

We did: both of us. It all happened so suddenly. And other things were happening, too. Indians were yelling and shouting and running in all directions. Most were rushing for the houses, or coming out of them with bundles of heavy muskets on their shoulders, and as many powder horns within their grasp. They ran to the beach, and there, at the water's edge, they knelt down with the butts of the muskets on the ground.

"Sails—the Indians are firing off muskets into the air," I cried, above the noise and confusion.

"Never mind 'em, lad," he called back. "Yell out! Ahoy! Rescue! Res-cue!"

By now, the Indians were lining the shore and firing muskets over the water. I was trembling violently, scarcely able to keep my grasp of the rigging. Out in the

Sound, the glint of a gun was followed by the cannon boom.

"Hurray!" shouted Sails, beside himself now. "They've got the guns manned. Let 'em have it, boys—give 'em the grapeshot," he yelled.

There was another glint, and another boom, which echoed and re-echoed in the Cove. But a minute later, the two ships appeared to lose heart, and to pause. The cannon spoke no more.

"They're close-hauling, Sails," I gasped out, sick at heart.

"*No!* By Davy Jones, no!" he bellowed, in baffled rage. "They can't do that. Can't the swabs see us?"

He was almost sobbing with anger, and his body seemed to sag.

"They're yeller, John!" he burst out again. "The swabs are yeller. They call themselves men, and they run away—away from a bunch of Indians!"

The crews of the two ships appeared to be manning the braces, turning the yards to the wind. We saw how the sails fluttered and shook; the masts leaned over; and the two ships swung around in their courses and stood out to sea.

"Get down, lad," said my shipmate.

We descended to the deck. At that moment, Maquinna's canoe, keeping close in to the shore, rounded the promontory at great speed and came into the Cove. There was no whale. Perhaps the harpoon had drawn, and the whale had got away; or, more probably, the arrival of the

43

ships had put an end to the hunt. We saw Maquinna step quickly onto the beach. We could see him ordering the Indians to return all the muskets within doors. So excited were they, that we heard the Chief raise his voice many times to quiet them.

"What shall we do, Sails?" I asked, fearfully.

"Reckon we'll give that lot a wide berth, lad. Reckon we'll drop into the boat, and get out of sight of the village, some way up the Sound. Then we'll think again."

"But the ships might come back, Sails."

"Maybe they will. Maybe they won't." His face was grim.

I ran below to get hold of some ship's biscuit and more chocolate to stuff in my pockets. Then I returned to the deck, ready to drop into the longboat.

"Sails, where are you?" I cried.

He was nowhere to be seen. I turned frantically about, looking this way and that. For one horrible moment I wondered if he had dropped overboard—or something worse. The ship was haunted with so many ghosts.

"Sails—Sails—Sails!" I cried.

And then he appeared, clutching something behind his back, almost guiltily. It turned out to be not a bottle of rum, as I might have expected, but a packet of writing paper from a locker in the Captain's cabin, and a pen and ink.

As quickly as we could, we dropped into the longboat, took up our oars, rowed with all speed away from the village in the shadow of the ship, and did not rest until we were out of the Cove and out of sight. We beached the boat in a concealed place, hurried through the trees to the high ground behind the village, and there we climbed into the branches of a large pine tree. Then, and not till then, did we relax, and draw regular breath.

7

What We Saw from the Pine Tree

From our position in the pine tree we had a good view of Maquinna's longhouse, and of the *Boston* anchored in the Cove, and of the more distant sea. We could therefore keep one eye on the activities of the Indians, and one eye on the possible return of the two ships. I felt sure they would come back. Sails was equally certain they would not. That's why he had snatched up paper, pen and ink to bring ashore. We were going to write letters, he said. And when we had eaten a good meal of ship's biscuit and chocolate, that's what we began to do. Thirsty as I was, Sails forbade me to drop to the ground and look for a freshwater stream.

"Are you ready, lad?"

"Well, Sails, sitting up in a pine tree isn't the best place for writing letters. But I'll try."

46

"I'll tell you what to write, lad. All you've got to do is to set it down so that others can read it."

"Others?" I asked.

"Sea captains and such," he said. "Now, begin. . . ."

I dipped the quill pen in the ink as best I could.

"*To any sea-captain what gets a hold on this letter . . .*"

I began to write. The pen scratched a great deal, and my position was most uncomfortable, but I soon looked up, ready for more, and Sails continued, "*. . . Please rescue two seamen, by name John Thompson, sailmaker, and the lad, John Jewitt, ship's blacksmith, both of the brig* Boston, *out of Boston, Massachusetts, what has got into the clutches of Indians with all our poor shipmates massacred. In God's mercy, come to our rescue.*"

I altered the letter a little in the writing, as seemed fitting, and read it back to him. Then we signed it, he with his mark, I with my full signature. He seemed pleased—if anyone in the plight we were in could possibly seem pleased.

"What it is to be a writer!" he said, enviously. "Lad, it's you is the lucky one, having a great skill like that. Now you copy out the letter again. One isn't enough. Write it twice—three times—four—as many times as you've a mind to, without straining your eyes. And we'll sign 'em and give 'em to the visitors Maquinna was telling us about—the ones he's expecting for a ceremony. And with every letter, lad, you'll give one of your daggers, as a present for being our postman. Any Chief who sails out of Friendly Cove, up the coast or down the coast, could take one of your letters. Sooner or later we'll get rescued that way." Sails stopped speaking for a moment. Then, "Look," he said.

Birds were fluttering in nearby branches. A blue jay screeched. But beyond this, down on the beach, the Indians were unloading the *Boston* at speed, carrying cargo ashore. Some of the men and boys were in the rigging, where they appeared to be moving about with the ease of experienced seamen. They were hacking at her spars and tops with axes, completely stripping her of sail.

It was now late afternoon. And there we sat, helplessly and hopelessly, concealed in our pine tree, saying little but seeing all. From time to time, we eased our positions, stretched our limbs, or moved cautiously to other forks of the tree, being careful not to disturb the outer branches. Now and again, whenever the pangs of hunger prompted us, we took biscuit from our pockets, or chocolate, and nibbled it. My shipmate also sucked at a pipe or chewed a quid of tobacco.

As night came on, torches were lit before the long-houses; fires flared up, and a feast began. We saw Maquinna and his men sitting on the ground, with bowls of food before them. The rest of the inhabitants were all around. Then, the eating over, Maquinna stood up to address his people. The torches lit up his figure against a dark and shadowy background. From time to time he paused in his speech, and a chorus of "He-yo, He-yo" broke from the listeners. He was doubtless telling his men what fine warriors they were, the takers of white men's ships. Then, when he had finished, the assembled Indians gave a great shout. My shipmate, hunched uncomfortably beside me in the branches, snorted with indignation. Over and over again, the shout rang through the air, disturbing the seabirds along the Cove, and startling the forest birds on their branches. Then the Indians raised rattles and drums above their heads, and created the most tempestuous din. And so it went on, far into the night, and we remained perched in our tree like two forlorn owls, watching it all, and wondering where it would end.

"They're going wild, Sails," I said.

"They've got something to go wild about, lad," he replied bitterly. "First they capture the *Boston* and her cargo; and now, this blessed day, they scare off two other brigs. Isn't that something to go wild about? They've had a lucky day."

"And we've had an *unlucky* one," I said.

"I suppose it can't be helped, lad," he replied, more reasonably. "We did all we could, you and me. We shouted hard enough. If those two brigs had turned great guns on 'em you'd have seen the Indians scamper into their houses like rabbits. And the ship's boats would have come to pick us up; the *Boston* would have been manned in a couple of shakes, Maquinna put in irons, and us away

49

to sea. Leastways that's what I'd have done, if I'd been captain. You know, lad, it's a lot for me to have to swallow—me, a man o' the Navy."

"I know, Sails. You served under Lord Howe."

"Aye. Black Dick, we called him; and a real sailor, he was. Twenty-six ships o' the line, the French had, off Ushant, on the Glorious First of June. Seven, we captured; ten we dismasted, and—"

"—and you were there, Sails."

"And I was there. And I wasn't sewing sailcloth in those days."

"You were gunner's mate."

"I was gunner's mate." He raised his voice, heedless and defiant. "And we didn't turn tail and run—like them stove-in rum puncheons this morning; my tongue forbids to call 'em brigs."

"They still might have second thoughts, and come back for us."

"Not them!" he spat out. "Not them! And can't you see the way it is, lad? They'll be speaking to all ships that come their way, telling them there's danger at Friendly Cove—warning 'em away."

He paused a while, and neither of us spoke. An owl hooted in the branches somewhere behind us. At last, after a heavy sigh, he spoke again.

"It's not so bad for you, lad. Live and let live, says you . . . Oh, yes, you do. The Indians have been wronged, says you, and we've got to forgive 'em for taking revenge on us. I saw you thinking that way, plain as

50

daylight. I saw you acting that way with Maquinna. Not me, lad. Don't you be expecting me to kowtow. No. I've fought the French, and I've fought the Spaniards, and now I'll fight the Indians. I believe in plain speaking, lad. They murdered our shipmates, and *that* I'll never forgive 'em."

I could see in the darkness the old man's fiery eyes burning out of that bristly face which he had brought close to mine. "Aye, by Davy Jones, I hate 'em," he smoldered on. "Lad—you see 'em down there, out in the open, with their torches blazing. Wait till they all go in, and the fires die down. Then we could do it."

"Do what, Sails?"

"Why—get down to yon brig in the moonlight; go aboard her; cut her adrift; and get her under a bit of sail while the breeze is offshore. What d'you say, lad?"

"Would we stand a chance, Sails?"

" 'Course we would."

"All right, then."

"That's the boy! That's the *Boston*'s blacksmith talking. We'll give 'em another hour or two, then we'll make our way to the longboat. It'll be tricky, but reckon we'll find it. . . ."

And so, with these thoughts and resolutions in our minds, the hours went by. We were cramped and stiff, edging ourselves gingerly into the forks of the tree formed by the branches, and trying hard to get rid of the numbness in our limbs. We even turned our backs on the village, by way of a change, and peered into the dark forest on the other side. Thompson sucked at his clay pipe, making it wheeze. And all the time, those words of the Captain kept running through my mind: "*I want no trouble with the Indians. . . .*" The Captain was now beyond all trouble, and the rest of the crew with him, I thought. We shifted our position in the tree, turning once more toward the longhouses and the sea.

Torches were burning in the village. Eating and speech-making had finished, and it looked as though the Indians were about to renew their labors of unloading by moonlight. Either that, or they were going after the rum.

We held our speech and watched as a score or so of them ran their canoes through the dark water. Some were holding aloft blazing torches, sputtering yellow and red flame, and casting an eerie light toward the ship. Almost at once the skimming canoes were alongside the *Boston*. First the torches were reflected in the ruffled water; then they were globes of fire moving up the ship's side; then fireflies, darting and dancing hither and thither about the deck.

"Look," shouted Sails, loud enough to be heard in the village. "Look, lad, they're going below deck—you can see the lights in the ports. By Davy Jones—blazing torches below deck! Blazing torches—and powder magazines down below!"

Even as he spoke, quickly spreading flames could be seen aft. "She's afire!" I shouted in alarm.

A cry went up from the beach, while out on the *Boston* the fire was spreading the length of the deck, catching at canvas, ropes and spars, and lighting up the surrounding water. The Indians were jumping from the ship now, with torches in their hands. We saw the torches sputter out as they touched the water.

"What about the powder, lad—the powder?" shouted my shipmate at the top of his voice. I shouted in reply, to tell him to keep a tight hold on his branch or he would fall. The blazing deck of the ship was now lighting up the sky, the Cove, the Indians' houses, the very branches of our pine tree.

"The powder, lad, the powder!"

Almost before the words were out of his mouth there was a flash, and a violent explosion that shook the tree in which we were perched and brought down a shower of pine needles over us. For a moment the dark sky glowed. A great shower of sparks and bits of sailcloth rose in the air above the burning *Boston*, and fell with loud hisses and spurts into the surrounding sea. Then followed another explosion, and another; and still another after a moment's pause, sending showers of burning pieces through the air, to fall flaming and floating on the water for a moment before dying out.

"She's a goner, lad," came the husky voice of my shipmate. "She's a goner, lad. She's finished."

"Our poor old ship," I said, near to sobbing.

"Aye. She's finished. We've seen the last of her. She'll be no more than a smoking hulk when daylight comes."

Neither of us spoke again for a very long time, as the ship burned herself out. And as the fierceness of her burning slackened, the noise and confusion on shore among the Indians fell away to a strange silence. The glowing ship darkened to a smoldering, smoking hulk, and finally slid under the water. My heart sank with her. Our last link with home was gone.

The moon had now disappeared, but the pale light of dawn crossed the sky; and a few birds chirped and sang in the trees. We stretched our stiff limbs, and lowered ourselves slowly to the ground. Then we made our way to a little lake, and sat on the bleached skeleton of a fallen tree at the water's edge. The colorful dawn sky was reflected in the clear water. If times and circumstances were different, I thought, how wonderful it would be to live beside this little lake, to swim in its clear water, or to fish from a small canoe.

A few ravens, not far off, were noisily devouring some prey—whether fish, or fowl, or water rodent we could not tell. They were making a hasty meal of it, flapping their wings, squawking, and tearing morsels away.

Where we were sitting, a small, freshwater brook emptied itself into the lake. I lowered my head into the brook and drank deeply of the cold fresh water. Sails followed my example. The food we had carried away with us from the ship was now all gone.

"I'm hungry, Sails," I said.

"Aye, lad, so am I," he replied.

We sat and watched the ravens gorging on their prey.

"What shall we do?" I asked, dolefully. He shook his head.

"Reckon we could fish—if we had anything to fish with. Reckon we could hunt, if we had a musket. Or we could pick up some clams and mussels down by the sea. But I guess, lad, we'd best swallow our pride, find the longboat, go back to the village, and beg for our breakfast."

8

The Gift-giving

If we could not escape, then *what*, in the name of mercy, could we do? We would have to try to live with the Indians, and be like the Indians. We would have to learn their language and follow their ways. We would have to work hard so as not to offend them—and to earn our keep. We would have to be ever on our guard, ever watchful, and, last but not least, ever hopeful of eventual rescue.

Thoughts like these, however, were soon pushed aside by the press of events: for we now found ourselves in the midst of great excitements; in the very center of an Indian Gift-giving.

Two days after the burning of the *Boston*, many Indians came to Nootka in canoes. They came from the north and from the south and assembled in the Cove, waiting to be welcomed ashore—hundreds of canoes, in line abreast, their occupants holding paddles aloft in salute.

On shore, lining the beach and cliffs of the Cove, were Maquinna's men, dressed in lengths of red, blue, or yellow cloth taken from our cargo. Powder horns and shot bags were hanging around their necks, and some of them were wearing women's dresses—smocks from the stolen cargo.

It was the strangest of sights. From time to time, Sails gave out great gusts and guffaws of laughter. And I must say I preferred these outbursts to the loud curses and threats which, since our captivity, had come more commonly from him. At the same time, I feared he might offend Maquinna by his hilarity, at our cost. But Maquinna seemed not to take offense. Perhaps he was too busy to notice. Certainly Tyee Maquinna had bestowed on my shipmate a very special duty.

"Tom-soon big man," he said; "Tom-soon shoot big gun."

"Aye, aye, Squire," replied Sails, with a wicked glint in his eye. "Gunner's mate, under Lord Howe, I was; and now promoted. You just give the word, Squire, and we'll bombard."

Sails took up his position beside the *Boston*'s cannon, now set up in front of Maquinna's longhouse. A gun crew of Indians stood beside him. Atop of all the houses other Indians waited with sticks in their hands, ready at the word of command to drum out a welcome on the roof planks. The women and children lined the fronts of

57

the houses, also with sticks. Maquinna, on his own house-top, held a central and commanding position, like a general in charge of his army. I stood at his side, the ship's speaking trumpet in my hand.

My view at that moment, from the housetop, was one of strange splendor and fantastic pageantry—below me, the yellow sand, the blue sea, and a backdrop of cliffs and distant mountains; in the offing the native visitors, all quite motionless in their canoes, waiting to be invited ashore. The only stir came from the black crows and ravens, encouraged by the stillness to descend and pick at scraps. The only voice to be heard was that of Sails, addressing himself to his small group of subordinate Indians around the cannon.

"Lay off, and stand back. Keep your noses out, can't you!" he rapped out once or twice. Then he signaled to Maquinna that all was ready. The next moment, Maquinna's speaking trumpet (or rather Captain Salter's) was bellowing the word of welcome across the intervening water:

"*Wau-kash! Wau-kash! Wau-kash!*"

This was answered by a great shout from the strangers, and followed by an unbelievable tumult and tempest of noise on shore. Those on the rooftops beat upon the planks with their sticks, while the women and children rattled upon the sides of the houses.

Another command through the speaking trumpet, and Maquinna's besmocked musketeers at the water's edge

58

held their muskets upright with the butts pressed on the sand, and fired them off, awkwardly and timidly. At the same time, my shipmate discharged his cannon, which so startled the musketeers in front of him that they flung themselves to the ground, rolling and tumbling about on the sand. For a moment or two it was all diabolical bang and explosion and danger. Where the cannon ball fell, or whether it caused any casualties, it was impossible to determine, so great was the din and confusion. It had certainly gone over the heads of the musketeers who now leaped to their feet to begin a song of triumph, running backwards and forwards as they sang, jumping into the air, and waving their muskets with a careless abandon.

Soon the visitors were coming in, and Maquinna was leading into his house as many as it could hold. One of the Chiefs, by reason of his features and fair complexion, looked more like a white man than an Indian. His name was Ulatilla, Chief of the Kla-iz-arts. In contrast to Maquinna's tribe, these visiting Indians seemed rather serious, even somber.

Inside Maquinna's longhouse, the fiber-cloth partitions were removed, to open it out for the feast. The Indian guests sat on the benches ranged around the walls of the house, to leave a clear space in the middle. Steam and smells of fish rose from some hot stones. This was the Indian kitchen.

Sails and I stood near Maquinna, eating nothing, for nothing was offered to us. Soon all the visitors were partaking of the feast, which they ate in comparative silence. At the same time, these visitors eyed—very narrowly, I thought—Sails and myself, the white prisoners. We were, I suppose, in their eyes part of the *Boston*'s cargo, possibly to be given away at this Gift-giving. After they had sized the two of us up pretty thoroughly, they turned their attention to the cargo of colored cloth and muskets and sheet metal piled up in a corner. Sunlight, shining through gaps in the cedarwood roof planks, fell on this large stack of colorful plunder, making it glitter and sparkle. But no one touched it.

Maquinna and his son, Sat-sat-sok-sis, were holding themselves proudly, with heads erect, for they were about to begin a ceremonial dance. The women were getting the boy ready for it. They wrapped a piece of yellow cloth loosely around him. This cloth jingled with tiny bells sewn all over it. Next, they produced a cap with a carved wooden wolf mask attached to it. This they placed carefully on his head. At the same time, three of Maquinna's under-chiefs, Tatooch, Toopashottee and Toowinnakinnish, wearing sea-otter mantles, stepped forward, scattering small, white feathers over the ground. This white down represented snow. They had baskets full of it. They even sprinkled some over their own heads and shoulders. I wondered if they were going to scatter it over all of us, and whether it would start everybody sneezing.

But now Maquinna stepped forward in his own splendid sea-otter mantle. He had a whistle in his mouth and a carved rattle in his hand. With this rattle, filled with pebbles, he kept time to a rhythmic sort of tune on the whistle, as he stepped out with a light skipping movement of the feet.

The ceremonial wolf dance had begun.

Maquinna and his three swaying under-chiefs danced around the floor. Then Sat-sat joined them. Around and around they danced, until at length the men sat down, and the boy alone took the center of the stage. Many times he sprang, with unbelievable agility, high into the air. Then he spun around on his heels, very rapidly, within a small circle. All the time the under-chiefs were drumming on a long, hollow plank and singing doleful songs, with the help of Maquinna. And at every pause, the women applauded by crying out in chorus, "*Wau-kash! Wau-kash! Tyee!*"

At length the dance ended and Maquinna began to hand out presents to his guests, in the name of Sat-sat-sok-sis, his son. One by one, the visiting chiefs stood before Maquinna; one by one, they gave the salutation, "*Wau-kash, Tyee!*" One by one, with fierce and surly look, they snatched the presents held out to them. That night, more than a hundred of the *Boston*'s muskets, as many looking glasses, about four hundred yards of cloth, and twenty casks of powder were bestowed as gifts. And in the giving of these gifts, Maquinna had asserted his supremacy over the coastal tribes. He was their lord.

It was well on into the night when the mighty Maquinna called Sails and myself to him. "We sleep," he said. "You *no* sleep."

Sails gave him a hard look. "Oh, we don't sleep, don't we. And why not, Squire, may I ask?"

"Men sleep in canoes. John, Tom-soon—no sleep. You watch. You take pistols—keep guard." He gave us each a brace of pistols, and watched us prime them.

So there we were, the two of us, white captives of these Indians, given pistols, and told to keep an eye on the visitors! The situation was, I suppose, quite comic, though we, the victims of it, were not much amused.

We went out into the moonlight and sat down in front of Maquinna's longhouse, one on each side of the cannon. Chief Ulatilla, the one who looked more like a white man, followed us out to look at the cannon and to touch it several times in awe and wonder. Then he moved off toward the shore, where his canoe was beached.

Sails whispered to me across the cannon, "Wait here, lad; I'll be back," and before I could remonstrate with him, he had followed Ulatilla into the misty darkness. Soon, the last of the Indians had left the longhouse, and all was quiet.

I waited anxiously for my shipmate's return, feeling a dreadful loneliness and fear come upon me. Then, as quietly as he had gone, Sails reappeared through the mist.

"The letters, lad," he whispered. "I found a postman."

And he took up his place of duty again, on the other side of the cannon.

I was so relieved to have him back that I was content not to question him. But in a little while I could not forbear to whisper through the mist, "Sails . . . who?"

"Why, Ulatilla," he whispered back.

All was quiet, save for the lapping of water on the beach, and the occasional hooting of an owl, or other cry from the forest. The moon looked coldly on. Now and again this moonlit silence was disturbed by the mournful cry of a loon, by the screech of a nighthawk, or by a cough from one of the sleeping Indians, curled up in a canoe.

It was sometime later that a low creaking or grunting sound set me trembling, and brought me to my feet. I looked over the cannon: and there was my gallant shipmate, stretched out upon the ground, grasping a pistol in each hand, with his arms crossed on his body. His eyes were closed, his mouth partly open; and he was snoring. I did not dare to wake him.

At last, the dawn began to break, and the mist to rise; and no one was more thankful for it than I.

During the morning the visitors departed; but long before they had gone, I had, upon request, placed four copper daggers, unobserved, into the hands of my worthy shipmate; and he, in his turn, had placed them secretly in the hands of Chief Ulatilla of the Kla-iz-arts. The postman had been paid.

63

For the next few weeks, the cannon was fired off twice daily, at dawn and at dusk, so that any lurking Indians in the forest might be warned not to attempt an attack. We secretly hoped it might attract a ship to our rescue, but none came.

Sails soon acquired fame and distinction as the creator of "the big noise." The Indians grew to fear and respect him for it. "Lay off that cannon!" was an order as imperious as any uttered by Maquinna, and just as promptly obeyed by any prying and inquisitive Indian. Only Sat-sat and the boys ever dared to tease him. Once he lost his temper with them. And this nearly lost him his life.

9

Storm and Tempest

After the Gift-giving ceremony, life at Nootka settled into a kind of uneasy calm. In the dark of the evenings, we gathered around Maquinna's hearthfire. The massacre still lay heavily on our hearts and minds; but whenever we referred to it, or indicated a wish to know more about it—in particular, to know more about the white crew whose previous treachery had brought it about—Maquinna closed up like a clam. I asked for the name of the offending captain and the name of the offending ship, but these, he said, he did not know, because he had been away from Nootka when the treachery was committed.

None the less, Maquinna talked freely about other trading captains on the coast. Captain Meares, he told us, had built a fort with a palisade around it, down by the brook, and he had given Maquinna a couple of pistols for the privilege. His men had dug a dock, and his Chinese carpenters had built a trading sloop in it.

Maquinna understood that some of the white men came from Britain, others from New England. The first he called "King George Men," or *Kintshaushmen*, the second "Boston Men."

"John—Tom-soon—tell about white men," said Maquinna, one evening. Darkness had fallen. The hearth-fires were lit. Sat-sat was at his father's side. Indian women were making baskets nearby; and a few sons of the under-chiefs clustered around.

"The great Chief of our country is King George," I said.

"I know," said Maquinna.

"My father know," said Sat-sat.

"King George was King when Captain Cook was here at Friendly Cove," I said. "He is still King. He has been King for forty-three years—for many many moons."

"John—Tom-soon, *Kintshaushmen?*" asked Maquinna.

"That's right, Squire," said Sails, smoking strong tobacco from his clay pipe.

"Yes," I agreed. "We are King George Men, though our ship belonged to Boston Men. In our country people make many blankets, many muskets, many ships. The ships carry the blankets and the muskets to trade in other lands across the seas. White men trade with red men. White men want sea-otter skins. Red men want blankets and muskets. White men wish to be friends."

"Some white men good. Some bad," said Maquinna. "Steal our furs. Take our land. Take our firewood. Take our fish. Soon, white men take all. But I, Maquinna, say *No*. If white man take—I, Maquinna, take. If white men kill—I, Maquinna, kill also."

My shipmate was about to reply, but at that moment he swallowed some tobacco smoke and was convulsed in a fit of coughing. When he had finished, Maquinna continued, more calmly and with dignity.

"White men hunt *mahak?*"

"Yes," I replied, "white men hunt the whale. They go in their ships, far to the north, and hunt the whales among the ice. In my home town—in the port of Hull, many ships are to be seen. They go north to hunt the whale." I showed him with the fingers of both hands —ten—twenty—thirty—forty—fifty—sixty ships and more.

"That is many ships," said Maquinna.

"Many ships," said Sat-sat.

"The blacksmiths make harpoons from iron," I said. "I have made harpoons myself. White men make harpoons of iron. Red men make harpoons of mussel shells. Red men's harpoons not strong. *Mahak*, the whale, escapes. White men's harpoons strong. They hold fast."

"John make harpoons for me?" asked Maquinna.

"John make for my father!" commanded Sat-sat.

"I will make harpoons for you," I said. "I will build a new forge with stones. I will make charcoal for fuel. I will use the ship's bellows which you brought ashore. And I will forge harpoons of iron for you, such as the white men use."

"That is good," said Maquinna.

"Is good," said Sat-sat, nodding his head.

"I will make daggers and harpoons for you," I said. "Tom-soon will make sails for your canoes, and shoes out of ship's hemp, and trousers out of canvas."

"That is good," said Maquinna.

"Is good," said Sat-sat.

My shipmate was puffing hard at his favorite clay pipe; it had a bowl molded into the shape of a grinning face. Some of the Indians had tried to beg it from him; others had attempted to steal it; and one or two had offered to buy it, using shells for money. The air was now heavy with strong tobacco smoke. Some of the women began to cough. One of the Indians got up and moved a roof plank to let out the smoke.

I think it was a relief to everyone when Sails took the offending pipe from his mouth in order to speak.

"Reckon I'll light the lamps, Squire," he said. These were the ship's lamps, which had been brought ashore and which now hung from the roof. When they were all lit, Maquinna's longhouse looked quite festive and gay. Sails made it his job to clean the lamps, refill them with whale oil, and light them at dusk. As soon as he had moved away from the fire to perform this task, Sat-sat and the other boys quickly clustered around me. I had been teaching them to say a few English words, and now they were eager for the lesson to continue. I pointed to my head.

"What's this?" I asked.

"*Tau-hat-se-tee* . . . head," said the boys at once.

I pointed to my eyes.

"*Kassee* . . . eyes," they said.

"And this—tied up in a pigtail?"

"*Hap-se-up* . . . hair."

I twitched my nose, and with a laugh they responded: "*Neetsa* . . . nose."

"These," I said, pulling at both my ears.

"*Parpee* . . . eeaars."

"And these?" (My teeth.)

"*Chee-chee*," they said. "Tees."

"And this?" (My tongue.)

"*Choop*," they replied. "Tonga."

Then, "John sing," they said. I sang a verse of the ballad, "The Bay of Biscay-O"; and with that, they jumped up to look for other diversions. They had had enough of "lessons."

I was aware of a sultriness which could not be blamed entirely on my shipmate's offensive pipe. There were no stars through the gaps in the roof planks; only a solid stillness of dark sky. There was no wind; only an unusual heaviness in the air. Maquinna, I thought, appeared a little apprehensive. At that moment, however, my attention was drawn to the boys who were following my

69

shipmate around, tugging at his trousers as he reached up to the lamps, and then darting out of reach as he turned on them. Sat-sat appeared to be leading them on.

"Lay off!" shouted Sails, sharply.

The boys jumped back, making impudent grimaces at him. But the moment he turned to continue his job, they were at their tricks once more.

"Lay off!" Sails shouted again, with greater anger. Maquinna looked up. I could see that my shipmate was losing his temper, and I began to wonder with some alarm how it might end. But the boys knew no caution. More willfully than ever, they awaited their chance, nipped in, and tugged at his sailcloth trousers, making him spill the oil and drop the can. Whereupon he lost his temper, clenched his fist, whirled around, and struck Sat-sat a glancing blow on the face.

It was so sudden that the boy did not even cry out. He spun around on his feet and fell to the floor. A nearby Indian sprang forward, but Sails felled him with one blow. At once, all was confusion. I saw Maquinna snatch at a musket and point it at my shipmate, shaking with rage. And I saw Sails stand foursquare, his feet planted firmly astride, to face Maquinna. He was wrenching his shirt open to bare his chest. At the same time, the hearth-fire near which he stood flared into darting flame.

"Shoot, you 'eathen; go on and shoot!" he shouted passionately. I was rooted to the spot, my feet unable to move; and Maquinna was fumbling for the trigger. At that moment, some of the spilled oil caught fire along the

70

floor, startling everybody—everybody, that is, except my stalwart shipmate.

"Shoot! I ain't afeared to die!" he bellowed.

By this time I had leaped up, gone forward, and flung myself in front of Sails, to cover him.

"No!" I shouted. "No! No!"

Sat-sat was now on his feet again and running toward me, stretching up his hands as though to shield my face. At this, Maquinna lowered his musket. Then followed a tense and silent drama in which no word was spoken. Sails stalked into a corner by the *Boston*'s cargo and sat, oddly enough, on a powder cask. As for me, I sat down on my bench with my head in my hands and my heart pounding. The Indians seemed to be gathering together in a group, as herds of animals do when they scent danger. More Indians were entering through the door, attracted by the commotion. And then, with the suddenness of a pistol shot, a new alarm arose.

There was a sudden flash, lighting up the interior with a pale green glow; and close upon it came a tremendous clap of thunder. For a second there was a fearful silence; then sharp, concerted cries of dismay filled the space. The next moment, rain fell with a deafening thudding on the rooftop; it was spurting and spilling through the crevices of the roof planks, pouring down the inside walls, hissing and sizzling as it fell on the embers of dying fires, drenching blankets and mats and bales of cloth. A sudden fury of wind hit the building so that it shuddered and rattled. The ship's lamps, hanging from the rafters, swung violently around, till they finally fell to the ground and sputtered out. A mighty gust swept through the doorway and sent mats and blankets flying through the air before it. The Indians were scrambling for the door, running out into the heavy, pelting rain; and I followed them.

Just as I reached the door, another flash of lightning lit up the Cove with an eerie green light. I could see the blurred pine trees over on the headland, and the cannon in the clearing, shining wet; and the Indians running helter-skelter in all directions, and climbing the notched corner posts of their houses to reach the flat rooftops.

Then all was black fury again. In what seemed like a mad game of follow-my-leader, I groped my way to a corner post and climbed to the roof of Maquinna's house. As I scrambled to the top, another flash showed up the figures of men grasping hold of the large roof stones for anchorage, lying flat and spreading their own weight to hold the roof planks down.

I followed their example. And as I lay there with my teeth clenched, my clothes drenched, and my hair and face running with water, I was, in my imagination, back again aboard the *Boston*, and battling through Cape Horn squalls on our voyage out.

I wondered where Sails was. The next lightning flash revealed him to me. He was in the clearing below, with rope and tarpaulin, lashing down his cannon, protecting it from the deluge.

72

At the same time I saw Sat-sat running from the house in his direction.

Then, I saw several things happening, all in a second, and lit up by the same lightning flash. With a clatter, I saw a roof plank lifted bodily by the gale and hurled through the air toward my shipmate and his cannon. He looked up, and saw it coming. He also saw Sat-sat, fleeing in the path of danger; and he hurled himself out of the way, at the same time heaving Sat-sat violently to one side with him, as the heavy plank of cedar wood crashed to the ground. It was the second time that my shipmate had done violence to the Chief's son. The first time, in his anger, he might have taken the boy's life; the second time, he almost certainly saved it.

At last, the storm abated, and a pale moon escaped from a black curtain of cloud to shine forlornly down. We descended to the ground of squelching mud and went indoors to a sodden and sleepless night.

10

Summer at Nootka

In June, the sun shone warm in the sky, the sea sparkled blue in the Cove, and the pine-sweet air was fresh and invigorating.

It was in June that I began my journal. I used a blank ship's account book, a raven's quill for pen, and berry juice mixed with a little finely-powdered charcoal for ink.

I began it sitting beside our little lake in the forest, where the freshwater brook flowed into it and fed it. Ferns and grasses and flowers, and singing birds were all about us. Hummingbirds twittered and buzzed in the bushes, preening feathers, or probing flowers for honey, or darting at intruders with angry squeaks.

Every Sunday, with Maquinna's permission, we came to this delightful place to wash ourselves and our clothes, and to pray for our deliverance; and I would write. The

Indians respected this Sunday privacy. They themselves sometimes wandered alone in the forest to pray to their god, Quahootzee, the Great Tyee of the Sky.

Only once was our privacy broken, and that was by Maquinna himself. He saw me carry out of the village the ship's account book in which I wrote my diary; and, being suspicious, he followed us at a distance. I sat down, as usual, at the edge of the lake in the shade of trees, my book open, my pen in my hand. Sails, as was his custom, was telling me what to write. And then, suddenly, without warning, Maquinna was at our side.

"John write bad of me," Maquinna said.

"No, no," I protested, emphatically shaking my head.

"If John write bad—I burn book," he said, and turning from us, he disappeared into the forest. He never repeated the intrusion; but from that day forth, I was obliged to write my journal in secret, at times when, and in places where, I was satisfied I could not be discovered.

It was Sails who had urged me to keep the journal in the first place.

"It will be evidence, lad," he said, "and we shall need that evidence for the ship's owners when we get rescued."

During those weeks of summer we were both kept busy. My shipmate spent many hours with his palm and needle. He sewed sails for Maquinna's canoes, and made trousers for both of us, a neat tunic suit for Sat-sat, and a cloak of many colors, from cloth samples, for Maquinna. As for me, I was employed mostly in making copper daggers. Mirror daggers, I called them, because I polished them so brightly that the Indians used them to look at themselves.

Whilst Sails was content to sit and sew his life away, to polish his cannon and the ship's lamps, I preferred to range more freely about the village. Muskets and fowling pieces from the *Boston*'s cargo were kept in all the longhouses by the under-chiefs. It was my job to go around, at regular intervals, to clean and oil them. This I was glad to do, because at the back of my mind was the thought that one day a ship would come and take us aboard; and this ship, I argued, would insist on taking up every item of the *Boston*'s plundered cargo, especially the firearms.

Sat-sat was often with me in my going to and fro, acting as guide. From him, I learned Indian words and Indian customs; from me he learned English words, and something about the ways of the white man.

Sometimes we watched the felling of the giant cedar trees in the forest. Very laboriously, the Indians felled them, using stone wedges. Most of their tools were of stone: wedges, chisels, adzes and mallets. For a drill they used a sharpened bone which they twirled in their hands. They used wedges not only to fell a giant cedar, but also to split it lengthways down the middle. They were always careful to choose trees of uniform thickness, with no branches. Then the long logs were dragged from the forest to the shore.

At Friendly Cove there were two skilled boatbuilders. They were rich. Their boats were famous up and down

76

the coast. Indians came from great distances to exchange large quantities of furs for a splendid Nootkan seagoing, whale-catching, war-making canoe. Fifty feet long, they were; and eight feet wide; magnificent to look at, whether riding the waves or beached and fastened to a paddle, which the Indians drove deep into the shore for a tying-up post.

With a tree trunk split lengthwise on the shore, the boatbuilder began the first rough work. Other Indians helped him in this. Wedges were used to remove large chunks of wood in order to get the first crude shape of the canoe. Then the boatbuilder used fire to char the wood, and this was then removed with a stone adze.

This tool, like a small chopper, was used for hollowing, shaping, and curving the craft.

Next, the boatbuilder filled the canoe with water, dropped large red-hot stones inside, covered the whole thing with large leaves of sea lettuce, and waited for it to steam up: then it would become soft and pliable. This was the time to insert sticks of varying length from one side of the canoe to the other, wedged between the gunwales, to keep the canoe bulging to the desired shape.

Next, the boatbuilder ladled out the water and allowed the canoe to dry. When it was dry, it kept its shape. To find if he had molded his canoe to an even thickness and balance, he bored holes through the sides with his bone drill, and inserted sticks to measure the thickness. Afterwards, he plugged these small holes with wooden pegs.

Last of all, he fixed the thwarts and the raised prow

and stern pieces. These were finely carved. They were pegged on, and for added strength, they were also sewn to the main body of the canoe with strong and supple cedar twigs and yew.

Sometimes the boatbuilders allowed me to give a helping hand, usually with the painting. The canoes were painted red inside, and charred black on the outside. The paint was made from red ocher, mixed with fish oil or whale oil.

Sometimes I helped to give the finish to the outside of a canoe. First, we used sharkskin to rub the wood reasonably smooth; and then we singed the surface with a cedar-bark torch, and left it in its charred black condition.

Paddles were made from yew or maple wood.

I sat for hours and watched the boatbuilders at their work; and Sat-sat was usually with me.

"Your boatbuilders are very clever men," I told him. "If you were to give me a stone chisel and a bone drill, and then ask me to build you a canoe, I would be quite helpless. 'No good.' I would say. 'John no good.' "

"White man no can build red man's canoe," he replied. "Red man no can build white man's ship." Then he said, "Once, white man build ship—big ship—there." He pointed to where the brook flowed into the Cove. Dogwoods with large white flowers grew beside the brook, but where it emptied itself into the sea, I had noticed what appeared to be relics and foundations of Captain Meares's blockhouse.

Out in the Cove, and beyond, in the Sound, Indians

were fishing in their canoes, with baited lines fastened to the handles of their paddles. Some of them were using the iron hooks I had made specially for them from nails; others favored the bone hooks of their own fashioning, fixed to lines of whale sinew and baited with sprat.

"Let's go fishing, Sat-sat," I said.

"Yes. *Ma-mook-su-mat;* go—to—fish," he said. And off we went, each in a small canoe of the kind already described.

The Cove was radiant with warm sunshine. I fastened my fishing line to the paddle handle, and with each paddle stroke kept the bait in motion. Around and around the Cove I paddled, a few canoe lengths behind Sat-sat; and then, when my mind was far away and thinking of home, the line unexpectedly tautened. With a shout of surprise, I hung on and heaved, almost overturning the canoe. And by good luck rather than good management, I hoisted a magnificent fighting salmon. I couldn't believe my eyes. But there it was—with a few gallons of cove water I had shipped in the process.

In these and other ways we spent our days out of doors. The Indians followed their summer occupations; my shipmate remained attached to his sailmaker's needle and palm; and I devoted myself to metal working whenever I was not fishing in the Cove, or gathering berries in the forest, or helping out with food or fuel or Indian crafts. But I made it my task, above all else, to look after the firearms, for the reason I have already given.

On many summer nights we slept out of doors, under

79

the cedars. And every Sunday, without fail, Sails and I went to our little lake in the forest, to wash our clothing; to swim and bathe and watch the hummingbirds; and to pray earnestly for our eventual deliverance from our Indian captors.

And so, as day followed upon day, and week upon week, the summer passed away. And then, one day—it was September 2, 1803, according to our reckoning—Maquinna called me to him and told me something which caused me to catch my breath with surprise.

"Tomorrow we go," he said.

"Go?" I asked. "Tyee Maquinna, I don't understand you."

"Go from Nootka," he said. "Go from sea."

I was completely taken aback. So this was the end, I thought. No ship had come to the rescue. After tomorrow, no ship would be any use to us. All hope of escape was gone.

II

September Migration

I ran at once to my shipmate. He was sitting on the headland, as he so often did, staring out to sea.

"Sails," I called to him as I ran up, "you won't like the news I have to tell you."

"What news?" he demanded. He was chewing a piece of coarse grass, held between his teeth.

"We are going away from Nootka," I said breathlessly.

He scrambled to his feet. "Who's going away from Nootka?"

"We are. All of us. The whole village."

"Where to?"

"Inland. Up the Sound. Away from the sea," I said, gaining my breath; and without another word, he stalked off toward Maquinna's longhouse. Maquinna, at his doorway, watched him come.

"Look here, Squire, what's all this about going away?" Sails demanded.

"Bad storms at Nootka. We go from sea," said Maquinna.

"Go where?" asked Sails roughly.

Maquinna pointed up the Sound. "One day in canoes," he said.

We went early to bed. For a long while I lay awake, wondering what the next day might have in store for us; then I must have fallen into a heavy sleep. At dawn, my shipmate's raucous voice wakened me; and I opened my eyes to find that the roof of our longhouse was already being removed.

"Wake up, lad," Sails was crying. "Wake up; there'll soon be no roof over your head."

Sails was right. The first streaks of dawn were crossing the sky, and I could plainly see them. Most of the roof planks had been moved to the ground.

We dressed and, without thought of washing or eating, we dragged our sea chests out of the house and down to where the *Boston's* longboat was moored. There we secured the small mast with its yard, and we fitted a new square sail made by my shipmate during the last few days. The gentle wind, blowing off the sea and up the Sound, would help us on our way and save us some hard work of rowing.

Our sea chests we stowed, one fore and one aft of the longboat. They gave the appearance of castles, fore and aft, as on the little ships of ancient times. Captain Salter's writing desk we also got aboard; then we ran the cannon down to the shore, and maneuvered it aboard the boat, amidships, with quoins, ammunition, powder and hemp round about.

"She looks like a little man-o'-war, Sails," I cried.

"You've only to say the word, lad, and we'll make her a *real* one," he said, jokingly.

An Indian dog was skulking nearby. It seemed to have become attached to my shipmate. Sails called to it now, in a voice of unmistakable authority.

"Come here! Come here, Jack!" he cried. The dog came slowly forward, tail between legs, making little dog-curtsies as it came.

"Sit down, Jack! Sit down, boy! Listen! You got to guard our sea chests."

The dog wagged its tail and licked my shipmate's out-stretched hand.

"Go on! Get aboard! Up! Up! On my sea chest! Up!"

It wasn't long before he had made the dog obey, and sit like a statue on top of the sea chest. My shipmate had a way with dogs.

By now, the village was all activity. Ravens were croaking; excited children shouting. It reminded me of a day, back home, when I had risen early to see the Hull Fair—the biggest fair in England—dismantle, pack up, and take the road for York and Newcastle.

All the roof planks were now removed and neatly stacked. Next, the loose planks from the ends and sides of the houses were lifted away, leaving only ridge poles, corner posts and intervening posts standing in the ground, like tree trunks denuded of branches, painted with rings of red and black.

Then, the Indians carried the planks down to the beach, and through the shallow water to the large canoes, already lashed together in pairs, abreast.

They loaded the first pair of canoes, putting down the planks with a proper balance, crosswise, to form a deck. Then, on this deck they loaded other planks, alternately lengthwise and crosswise, up to a height of six or eight feet, leaving space only at the prow and the stern sufficient for an Indian with a paddle in his hand. Such was the strength and structure of these canoes that they could hold this great load and still remain seaworthy.

When all the house planks had been loaded in this way, the Indians turned their attention to the village furniture, the tubs and baskets in which they kept all their goods; and finally to what remained of the *Boston*'s cargo, which was considerable.

Long before noon, the Indians had struck camp; the mothers had fastened the babies in their cradles and the cradles on their backs; the families had climbed atop the loaded planks; and with a loud chorus of song we left Friendly Cove. Maquinna's canoe went first, then our longboat with the Indian dog still sitting on my shipmate's sea chest, and after us a long line of crowded and freighted canoes. As I glanced back at the place we were leaving, the village site looked like some blighted and fantastic woodland, given over to the crows and ravens

which had already alighted there to quarrel greedily over
their scavenging.

Loud was the singing, and gay the procession up the
Sound, as we made our way by tree-lined shores toward
the distant scarred peaks and wooded mountains, until
the sun began to set and a large hunter's moon climbed
the darkening sky. All through the night the dusky con-
voy plied slowly ahead, scattering waterfowl, and disturbing frogs and fishes. Some of the babies cried in the
night. Some of the children slept. But the men and
women took turns at the paddles, chanting rhythmically
in time to the splashing of their paddle strokes. Two Indian slaves were put aboard the longboat to give Sails and
myself rests at the paddles. Even so, we were exhausted
by our unaccustomed labor.

When dawn came, and mists like floating veils lifted
and disappeared, I saw that we were in a channel between high mountain scenery. At every turn of the head,
a new romantic view presented itself: lofty mountains;
tall, dark spruce and fir; maples ablaze with golden au-
tumn foliage; and leaping cascades of water, sparkling in
the morning sun.

At length, we reached the very end of our water channel, into which rushed a rapid freshwater stream, not na-
vigable by the canoes. I saw a flat plain before me, not as
large as the Nootka clearing, but with the same solid
posts and ridge poles awaiting us. The only difference
that I could see was an absence of crows and ravens and
the welcome presence of lush meadow grass, which was a

surprise to me for the time of year. And behind this plain, standing up bold and sheer, was a high mountain to shelter us from winter storms and cold.

By nightfall—though you would scarcely believe it possible—we had unloaded all the canoes, set the wide cedar planks in place around the posts, heaved heavy boulders up on the roof to hold the planks in place, and measured out our apartments, hanging them with matting as before.

Outside was the song of cascading waters, fresh and clear, falling down the mountain, and—more important at the moment—the smell of cooked fish and the sight of ripe red berries gathered by the women and children. How I enjoyed that first meal at Maquinna's inland village of Tashees!

Next day, we were up with the larks, if larks they were, which roused us with bursts of song from the first glimmers of dawn. Everyone, young and old, was up and out in the mellow sunshine. Children played; dogs barked; the waters tumbled and sang.

And now, odd though it may seem, we two survivors of the *Boston*, two castaways as you might say, began to enjoy life. Since no ship could reach us at Tashees, we were free of the strain of watching out for one.

We went salmon fishing. There were several rapids and waterfalls within sight of the village; and before long, the Indians had fixed cane lattice weirs below them all, with platforms to stand on, and dip nets to scoop up the salmon trapped by the weirs. What sport we had!

And what quantities of salmon were brought in, for the women to dry and cure. Salmon was our staple food: like bread in England. It was also wealth, because the Indians could trade it with less fortunate tribes.

We often went out with fowling pieces too; there were wild duck and teal. On Sundays, as at Nootka, we found a quiet, secret place for our devotions.

12

The Winter Ceremony

One day, Sat-sat-sok-sis told me about the salmon. *So-har* was the Indian name. He said the salmon were people— people who lived in villages under the sea; and that every year the salmon people sent young men and women, disguised as fish, to visit the Indians, whom they regarded as friends.

"But is it friendly to catch them and eat them?" I asked. "Don't they mind being caught?"

He said they didn't; and that as soon as they were eaten, the salmon became people again in their village under the sea—except for those whose bones had been eaten by dogs. For those, alas, died. And he warned me never to be careless enough to leave salmon bones lying about on the ground for the dogs to get.

"I will remember," I said; "and I will tell Tom-soon to remember also."

And this I did, a few days later, when my shipmate and I found ourselves alone together, in a new set of circumstances. It happened that all the women went into the forest to gather berries. Armed men went with them to protect them. Sails and I were told to join the party, and we were glad to do so. We took the ship's axes with us. At night, we kindled fires, and built rough shelters out of pine boughs. Sails and I shared a small shelter of our own, made with a few poles and a canopy of branches and foliage. My shipmate smoked his pipe and yarned about old times; and I took the opportunity to tell him of the strange Indian beliefs about the salmon, and to warn him about his disposal of salmon bones after a meal. He declared it "a fishy story" and laughed heartily, but promised to remember.

We remained in the forest for three days. Then, with our baskets full, we returned to the village, to press the berries between planks of wood, dry them, and store them for the winter.

On a day in December there occurred the first of a very strange set of events. At break of day, a hunting party went into the forest. The men wore moccasins up to their knees, and elk skins around their bodies, fastened with cedar thongs. They took dogs with them, and bows and arrows.

"What are they going to hunt, Sat-sat?" I asked.

"They hunt *Moo-watch*."

"What is *Moo-watch*?"

For answer, Sat-sat took a carved wooden mask of a

89

bear from a basket, put it on, and proceeded to imitate the awkward dancing movements of a large brown bear.

"I see. *Moo-watch* is the bear. Is *Moo-watch* fierce?"

"Not now. *Moo-watch* is fat. She is fat on berries and sah-mon. Hunters look for her in caves. Then they attack with dogs."

The next day, the bear hunters returned. The children saw them and shouted with excitement.

"*Moo-watch! Moo-watch! Moo-watch!*" they cried. "Here comes a bear—a bear!"

The hunters entered the clearing, carrying a large brown bear which they had killed. They took it into Maquinna's house, and the entire village followed, crowding around the door and filling up all the space inside. The men propped up the dead bear in a seat in front of Maquinna. And then some strange things happened.

First, Maquinna gently placed on the bear's head a conical, sugar-loaf hat, made from cedar bark. Next, he sprinkled white down and feathers on the bear's fur to represent snow. Then Maquinna called for a tray of food to be placed before the bear, and when this was brought, Maquinna, by words and gestures, invited it to eat.

"Well, lad, what d'you make of that?" mumbled my shipmate at my side. I did not reply, but gazed in wonder at this strange ceremony, which ended by the bear being skinned and a banquet prepared. A scene of joy and feasting followed, in which Sat-sat was called upon to repeat the masked dance I had seen.

This bear ceremony was but the beginning of the long winter ceremony in honor of the god of these Indian tribes. They called their god Quahootzee, the Great Tyee of the Sky. The next ministration to this god began in a manner so surprising that it startled me out of my wits.

It was the morning of December 13. Outdoors winter reigned. In Maquinna's house the central fire was kept at a good blaze. I was sitting near it, and Sat-sat, a few feet away, was deep in his own thoughts. Suddenly Maquinna took a pistol in his hand, strode up to his son, and fired the pistol close to the boy's ear. For a moment I was shocked and stunned. Then I jumped to my feet and shouted out a horrified protest.

"Stop!" I shouted. "What are you doing? Are you killing him?"

Maquinna ignored my interruption. Sat-sat had fallen to the ground as if dead, though I knew that this could not be so, because Maquinna had fired the pistol upward, at the roof. I could only conclude that Sat-sat had fainted with shock. Or perhaps he was *pretending* to be dead. . . .

It had all happened so quickly and unexpectedly. The women began to wail. Men rushed into the house, armed with daggers and muskets. I ran up to Sails who was looking at Maquinna with a fine disdain.

"What are they doing, Sails?" I whispered. "Please tell me what they are doing."

"Don't ask me, lad. You understand these crazy Indians better than I do. Reckon we'll disappear through the door."

But through that very door, not ten yards from us, there now entered two Indians dressed in wolfskins and wearing wooden wolf masks on their heads. They came in on all fours, lifted Sat-sat from the ground, and carried him off on their backs, out of the house.

And there we were—watching it all—our faces blank with amazement, until Maquinna, in a stern voice, called us to him.

"John—Tom-soon, go! Go from this house. Go from this village. Go into forest. Stay in forest seven days. If you come back before seven days, I kill you. If my men see you, they kill you. Go."

Without loss of time, as you can well imagine, we gathered up a few things, withdrew from the house, and began to follow a track up the forested mountainside. Then, when we had put some distance between ourselves and the village, we sat down to think.

Sails seemed almost unconcerned by what had happened. He was never surprised at anything the Indians did. For myself, I was uneasy and perplexed. I hoped that Sat-sat had suffered no hurt. It was, I supposed, some kind of Indian rite—a winter ceremony, as full of meaning to them, perhaps, as Christmas is to us. Yet I was tormented by doubt and uncertainty.

After a while, we got up again and followed the track through the trees, up the mountainside. Then my shipmate suddenly stopped, and took cover behind a tree, pulling me with him.

"What is it?" I whispered in sudden alarm.

He was listening intently. I listened too. But all I could hear was the thumping of my heart, and our breathing, fast and deep. Then I thought I heard a faint rustling of leaves a few yards down the track we had so recently covered.

"Are we being followed?" I whispered.

"Ssh . . ."

Again, I heard the rustling leaves; and at the same time Sails gave a noisy guffaw. "Followed? Reckon we *are* followed—by my friend, Jack." And with a bound, the Indian dog—the dog which had guarded so faithfully my shipmate's sea chest—was upon us, and jumping joyfully up at Sails.

"Well, well, well, if it isn't Jack!" he cried, in obvious delight at the reunion. "All right. All right. That's enough. Down, boy! Down!"

A harsher tone of voice brought immediate obedience from the dog.

"You don't think . . ." I began. "You don't think, Sails, that others are following us, and using the dog to get our scent?"

"I doubt it," he said. Then he looked at the dog. "What d'you say, Jack?"

The dog barked up at him.

"He says 'no,' " said Sails. "Let's go."

The three of us continued on our way. At length, we reached a place somewhat more open, with a rocky shelter or cave, cunningly concealed, and large supplies of dead or fallen branches all around. There we stopped.

"Forget your worries, lad," said Sails, in a voice that cheered me at once. "This is where we camp. You gather branches for a lean-to; I'll get a fire going." He took a tinderbox from his pocket. "And Jack, boy, you go out hunting and bring us back some supper."

The Indian dog barked; I laughed; and a woodpecker, a little way off, beat a cheerful tattoo on some forest tree.

13

Alone in the Forest

It was comfortable around the campfire, after a meal of forest game caught by Jack, prepared by Sails, and roasted on a spit by me. The Indian dog sat between us, wolfing any part of the repast that we threw to him.

Darkness came down, and the calls of wild animals and birds broke the stillness of the forest night. Sails took one of his few remaining clay pipes from his pocket, filled it with selected dry leaves, and puffed away to his heart's content. He had long ago consumed his stock of tobacco, but he managed very well on a variety of local substitutes. Occasionally he would become convulsed with raucous coughing, and once a small explosion in the bowl suggested that a few grains of gunpowder had by some mischance got into the mixture.

"Did you bring the logbook, lad?" he inquired, between puffs.

Yes, I had brought my journal, picked up hurriedly at our departure, and smuggled under my jacket.

"Then you get busy on it," he said.

He was a true seaman. The entries in our journal were as important to him as eating and sleeping. I did as he bade me, feeling very tired.

When I had finished, he built up the fire, damped it down with dead leaves and moss to make it last the night, and then we all three fell asleep, Sails and I with our feet to the fire, and the dog between us.

Early next morning, I was wakened by the growling of the dog. I sat up, feeling somewhat cold, and stiff in the joints. Sails was still fast asleep. He was snoring loudly. But the dog was on his feet, bristling, and continuing to growl in his throat. His head and eyes were directed beyond the campfire, which still smoldered and glowed among a heap of ash and sent up a thin wisp of whitish smoke. I rubbed my eyes, and stared out over the fire to the thin morning light filtering down through the trees. And then I froze in terror.

A large brown bear was not ten yards away, sniffing the ground. Fortunately the fire was between us. Even in my fright I told myself, almost calmly I think, to be thankful for it. The fire, at least, was some protection.

There I remained, still and staring, for a great length of time, it seemed. Jack continued to growl in his throat, Sails to snore in his sleep, and the huge bear to sniff. And then, several things happened at once. A spurt of flame suddenly leaped from the fire, as it collapsed and fell in

96

on itself. A flurry of spreading smoke rose into the air. The bear bounced back in surprise; the dog began to tremble violently; and Sails woke up, grabbing the dog by the scruff of the neck as he did so.

"What's up?"

He sat up, to see the bear making off down the track with a sprawling, rambling gait. The dog was straining to get away, choking in a paroxysm of hysterical barking. At last Sails released him, and he sprang away, swerving around the fire, and tearing down the track after the bear. As if by some primitive hunting instinct, we followed, grabbing hold of sticks. We ran and stumbled after the bear and the dog for something like half a mile, when the barking either ceased or was too far away for us to hear. We put our heads to the ground, but all was silent. Only a shrieking jay in a tree above us disturbed the silence. We rested, panting, for some time; then got to our feet, and tried to retrace our steps.

We came to a small mountain stream, falling over a cleft of rock. The water fell into a rocky basin where it was clear and fresh. We drank deeply. Then we washed, and felt better. A rather pale sun began to filter through the trees. We were sitting, looking up through the branches at an eagle hovering above, when a stirring of the undergrowth immediately beside us made us jump to our feet; and it was Jack who burst upon us, panting, his tail between his legs and a guilty look in his eyes. But he appeared to be quite unharmed by the bear.

"Well, well, boy," said Sails, with evident pleasure, "so

you've come back. And what did you do with the bear, eh?"

The dog's tail began to wag.

"Did you kill it?"

The dog licked his hand.

"I reckon you thought better of it, boy, and ran away."

The dog snuggled up to him.

"I reckon he was too big for you, eh, boy?"

Jack jumped up to lick his face; and all was well. We followed the brook upstream; and came at length to our camping ground. There we built up a fire, gathered more fuel for it, sat around it, and fell into discussing the art of trapping and the ways by which we might hope to feed ourselves royally for the remainder of the week.

It was wonderful to be free of the Indians, and on our own. We even discussed the possibility of making a run for it.

"Well, lad, I can see points for it; and I can see points agin it," Sails said. "Trappers we could become; backwoodsmen, living the life of the wild. Maybe we could start up a trade in furs. . . ."

"But sooner or later Maquinna would get us," I said.

"Him, or some other Indian varmints."

"We are his prisoners, Sails."

"Aye, prisoners on parole, that's about what we are. We *could* escape. There's nothing to stop us. We could make a run for it. But we wouldn't get far. It's a big country; there's a lot of forest. Trouble is you can't live in it forever. Not unless you're a squirrel. And you can't move about much unless you keep to the tracks. And the Indians who made 'em also use 'em; so you're bound to meet 'em from time to time. . . ." Sails was silent for a minute, thinking.

"You know, lad," he went on, "I sometimes think it would pay us if Maquinna was to sell us to another Chief —farther down the coast. We'd stand a better chance of a ship farther down the coast."

"From what Sat-sat told me, we shall be on the move again soon, anyway," I said.

"Back to Nootka?"

"No. Halfway back to Nootka. To a place called Cooptee—for the herring fishing. From Cooptee," I went on, "we shall return to Nootka, at a guess, at the begining of March. In fact, the very time of the year the *Boston* put into Nootka Sound. . . ."

We were both quiet for a moment, and Sails nodded.

"Aye. Last March, lad. Middle of March, it was, she tied up," he said.

"And let's hope we shall return this March to see another ship like her, anchored in Friendly Cove."

"Aye, you've got to be writing some more letters, lad. Waste no time talking. Start now. Then—one day . . . you'll see, lad. One day there'll be a ship beating into Friendly Cove, skimming down like a swallow, and sounding off her cannon; and she'll take us aboard, both of us, you and me."

14

Return

We returned, after our seven days of banishment, to the village, which we entered, with some caution, at evening time. All was quiet. Life had returned to normal. And what gave me the greatest mixture of pleasure, surprise and relief was to find Sat-sat-sok-sis very much alive and well. He welcomed us back, and gave us good seats at the hearthfire, where my shipmate at once took out a pipe and settled down to smoke and cough. It was almost as if we had never been away.

Our return was just in time for us to spend Christmas Day in Maquinna's house. I sang Christmas carols, just as I had sung them, in earlier years at home, sitting by the fireside. They always said I had a good voice at home; and even the Indians would listen without interruption to an English ballad and ask for more.

I told them about Christmas: about the Shepherds, and

about the Three Kings; and of the star which led them to the Babe, born in a manger, born to be King. They looked up at the dark sky through the gaps in the roof planks.

"Which star?" they asked. "Show us the star."

"It was the brightest star in the sky," I said.

Outside, the snow began gently to fall. Silence and peace were all around, so different from the earlier excitement and disturbance which had driven us so suddenly into the forest.

In the following days, I fell to wondering about that Indian winter ceremony, and what it could mean. Sails said it was black magic.

I think now that the performers in this seven-day ritual belonged to a secret society within the tribe. If so, only the richest belonged to it. Sat-sat once spoke to me —though guardedly—about what he called a Black Spirit which gave them power to stand any kind of pain without feeling it. It was difficult to understand. But when Maquinna fired that pistol shot, and Sat-sat collapsed on the ground, Sat-sat was perhaps being initiated into the secret society. When he was carried out of the house by the wolf-men, he would be taken to a secret place to be left on his own, so that he could be visited by the Black Spirit and given supernatural powers. Secrecy was so important in all this, I concluded, that I could well understand Maquinna's urgent need to send us away for the duration of the ceremony.

During the weeks of winter, we settled into the slow

rhythm of Indian life. The days, which were short, we spent in the woods, shooting game and gathering firewood. The nights, which were long, we spent round the hearthfires, trying our hand at carving and weaving, at dancing and song. And then, quite soon, at the end of January, we were migrating again. We moved down the Sound to Cooptee, a sheltered spot with a high mountain behind us. There, we fished for herring. The water was thick with them. We fished in pairs, one paddling the canoe, the other using a many-pronged fork to scoop the herrings into the boat. It was almost like haymaking, except that the harvest was of herrings.

We had herrings for breakfast, fried on hot stones. The Indians ate them throughout the day. I asked Maquinna why his people ate so much at Cooptee.

"When there is much, we eat much; when there is nothing, we starve," Maquinna said. "The moons of plenty are here. We eat much. Tom-soon eat much. John thin; Tom-soon thin also."

"That is because we feel the cold," I said. "Your people wear few clothes. King George Men wear many clothes."

"Too many," said Maquinna. "I wish John, Tomsoon, live like my people; look like my people; be my people."

"But if we are cold, we shall become ill," I protested.

"Soon we go to Nootka," he said. "Nootka not cold."

And sure enough, at the end of February, we dismantled our houses, loaded the house planks on the canoes, and returned to Friendly Cove, near the open sea.

Imagine our excitement at seeing the ocean once more. Imagine the hope and expectation that rose in our hearts. But, alas, throughout the whole long summer we saw not a single white man's ship. We looked always out into the Sound, and beyond to the open sea. Every day we searched hopefully the distant horizon. But never a ship came near to Friendly Cove.

We bore our affliction as best we could, and never gave up hope of eventual rescue. We also applied ourselves, as best we could, to the pattern of Indian life. We fished, worked at our forge, and went, every Sunday, to our lakeside retreat, to wash our clothes, and to watch the hummingbirds.

During that summer, two things occurred of particular importance, and these I must now speak about.

To begin with, there was Maquinna's lack of success in whaling. So failing in prowess was he throughout the summer that his under-chiefs made little effort to disguise their displeasure; and Maquinna himself was unable to hide his distress. It was a serious matter, because the unwritten law of the Nootka Indians decreed that the Tyee of the village should strike the first whale before others could join in the hunting; and this Maquinna failed to do. Moreover, for our part, we learned of a growing suspicion in the minds of the Indians that Sails and I had brought ill luck upon the village. There was indeed no lack of evidence of the growing hostility towards us. Sails especially received angry scowls and buffetings; though he usually gave as good as he got, and was always shouting oaths at them, quite unashamedly.

All this was bad enough, but another and far worse affair must now be mentioned, namely the slaying by Sails, in a fit of temper, of a Wic-an-an-ish Indian.

Chief Wic-an-an-ish and his Indians lived southward from us, about fifty miles down the coast. From time to time they visited Nootka, a day's voyage in a fast canoe; and it was on the last of these visits that there befell the misadventure of which I speak, though it is an event I do not like to think about, much less to put into words.

Sails, who was a great believer in cleanliness, had washed Maquinna's blankets in the brook, and had spread them out upon the ground to dry. Whereupon along came one of the Wic-an-an-ish Indians who stepped upon the blankets, looking at Sails with a leer on his face as he did so. I saw it all, since I was standing at my forge nearby, and hearing my shipmate's cry of anger, I looked up. With an oath, Sails upbraided the mischievous Indian.

"If you do that again, I'll kill you," he growled; and though the Indian did not comprehend his words, I could see at once that he meant them. I saw the foolish Indian trample in the mud and dirt, then jump upon the blankets again, to do a kind of dance on them. At this, my poor shipmate became enraged beyond control. He picked up a cutlass and smote the man's head clean from his body. I leaped forward, but the horrid deed was done.

A noisy crowd gathered around the hideous scene. Maquinna, who had seen what happened from a distance, came at once to the defense of Sails. He remonstrated at great length with Chief Wic-an-an-ish and his men. What Chief Wic-an-an-ish really thought about it, we could only guess, for he departed at once, with his men, and with the body of the victim. We were not sorry to see them go.

And we were not sorry, two days later, to make our own departure from that scene of violence and bloodshed; for the time had come to leave Nootka on our second winter migration up the Sound—to Tashees and the winter ceremony of the Indians.

But this time, we were forewarned and forearmed. At Tashees, with Maquinna's consent, we equipped ourselves with food and clothing, axes and fowling pieces; and with Jack, the dog, at our side, we strode up the forested mountainside until we reached the selfsame spot where we had camped, a whole long year before.

15

"A Year Older and a Year Wiser"

Back again in the forest, it was surprising how quickly we lopped off branches, drove stakes into the ground, and built up a tolerable shelter, using the Indian method of managing without nails. Next, we gathered quantities of dry leaves to make beds, and lastly, we kindled a large fire in the opening, which gave warmth and cheer to our forest abode.

We sat down on our leafy beds, with our feet toward the fire, and Jack sitting between us; and we ate a meal. This done, Sails took out his last clay pipe, broken at the stem. He filled it with a few selected dry leaves, and puffed away.

"A whole year has gone by, Sails," I was saying. "A whole year has gone by, and we are back again in this forest, sitting on the selfsame bit of ground."

"Aye," replied Thompson, nodding his head, "we're

both a year older, and a year wiser; and I've got rheumatism in my bones."

Poor old Sails! He had suffered badly from it for several months; and the pain didn't improve his temper. He pulled a sea-otter mantle around his shoulders, and kicked the fire to make it flame. There was a chill in the air. Sails was wearing the fur cap which he had made for himself. I was wearing a fur headband. I suppose we could easily have been mistaken for two real Indians. After almost two years of living among them, this is not surprising. We allowed our hair to hang loosely to our shoulders, as the Indians did, using a headband to keep it in place.

"You get busy on the logbook again, lad," Sails said, curling up his toes before the fire, and watching the wood-smoke rise.

I took the ship's account book from the bottom of the woven basket given to me by an Indian girl to use as a pack. I had brought my raven's quill pen with me; also the homemade ink I carried in a small ship's flask.

I made an entry to cover the last few days, while Thompson sucked at his pipe and kept his peace. Once or twice I felt his eyes upon me, watching me closely, as I recorded his killing of the Wic-an-an-ish Indian. I paused for a moment and looked toward him.

"Put it all in, lad," he said. "A logbook ain't a true logbook unless you do it right."

I read out to him what I had written and closed the book.

"Wait," he said. "While you have it out, best write a few more letters. It's easy out here with nobody a-watching you, except old Jack here, and the blue jays."

I pointed out to him that we had just gone through a whole summer without seeing a single ship, and that to write still more letters *"To any sea-captain into whose hands this letter might fall"* seemed a waste of time. But he wouldn't hear of it, and he harangued me like any schoolmaster.

"Listen to me, lad," he said fiercely. "You put that pen down a minute and listen to me. We didn't see a ship, says you. Why didn't we see a ship? I'll tell you. Because the *Boston* was captured by the Indians, and by now the news has gone around the world. They know about it in Canton. They know about it in London and in Hull. They know about it in Boston, Massachusetts. All the owners of trading ships know about it. 'Give Nootka a wide berth,' they say. 'Keep clear of Nootka for a year. Let the trouble die down.' But they'll come again in the spring. If you want to trade you have to take risks. You mark my words, lad, they'll be putting in to Nootka again this spring. And we've got to be ready for 'em— with letters, and plans for escape. And that's where Squire Maquinna comes in."

He paused only a moment for breath, and to push away Jack, who was licking his face. Then he continued as fiercely as before. "Maquinna's in a fix, lad. He's in a fix with everybody. He's in a fix with Wic-an-an-ish and the other tribes because they blame him for stopping the trade. He's in a fix with his own people because he's getting too old to harpoon whales. He's in a fix with us because we shall know too much about the massacre when the next trader puts in to Friendly Cove. But I reckon we're his best friends, you and me, as things stand."

"And for that matter, he is *our* best friend," I put in. "He and Sat-sat; Sat-sat especially."

This was true enough. Like us, Sat-sat was also a year older and a year wiser. He had grown. He was more manly and responsible in his ways. He was our friend and supporter.

"You're right, there," said Sails. "You're dead right. Without them two, we'd have been scalped long since, and that's the truth."

He stirred the fire with his foot, refilled his pipe, and relapsed into silence. So I copied out a few letters on the back pages of the account book, tore them out and handed them to him. He folded every one carefully; then he put them safely away in a pocket of his canvas jacket.

We slept well that night, and on every succeeding night. We had, indeed, a pleasant sojourn in our forest retreat, being in turn woodsmen, hunters, fishers and explorers. We tracked down game—raccoons, martins and squirrels—until, startled by our unexpected presence, they scurried along branches out of sight, or over the matted pine needles, to lose themselves amid low bush and scrub. Always we carried our axes on our excursions, and whenever we saw a danger of losing our tracks, we sliced a chip off the trunk of some prominent tree as a mark to guide us on our return. And back in our rustic abode, we made ourselves snug and warm in the bonfire glow. I sang songs of old England for the entertainment of my shipmate, and he yarned by the hour for mine. I am sure that our little midwinter camping holiday, in the crisp, invigorating air, away from the company of our captors, did us both a power of good.

Our return came a little sooner than expected. It was in the afternoon of our seventh day of banishment, when we were sitting by the fire, making plans to return the next morning to the village, that our attention was suddenly drawn to the dog beside us.

Jack became tense in all his limbs, scenting the air and snarling. The memory of the bear of the year before put me instantly on my guard, and I peered out, over the fire. And at that very moment, there came into sight, hurrying toward us, not the bear but Sat-sat-sok-sis himself. He strode up to us, out of breath.

"Sat-sat," I cried, in surprise. The dog relaxed, and sat down.

"John, Tom-soon," said Sat-sat, "my father say— come."

I looked at him, open-mouthed with astonishment.

"Is there trouble?" asked Sails.

"Yes, trouble."

"A raid?"

"No raid."

"What then?"

"Wic-an-an-ish and his men come in their canoes. My father say you help him. Come!"

We gathered our belongings together and followed him toward the village.

16

Wic-an-an-ish

It was with fear and foreboding that I followed Sails and Sat-sat, in Indian file, down the mountain path. Alarming thoughts entered my head. Wic-an-an-ish and his men awaited us and what could that mean? It could mean only that he had come at last to seek vengeance, or to demand retribution, for Sail's murder of one of his men.

I thought I knew Wic-an-an-ish and his ways. He had been jealous of Maquinna from the start. He was a younger man, the son of the Wic-an-an-ish who, with Maquinna had welcomed Captain Cook to Nootka in the year 1778. He had taken his father's name at the age of twelve, when he became head of his father's whaling canoe. He was strong. He had refused to attend Maquinna's Gift-giving, for fear of losing face. He and his men were no strangers to us. More than once, at Friendly Cove, he had taken Sails and myself to one side, trying to bribe us with promises of better treatment if we would leave Maquinna and join him. But we thought we knew well enough the story of the frying pan and the fire, and kept out of his way. More than once, Maquinna had confided in me that he feared it might come to war between them. More than once, Sat-sat had told me that Wic-an-an-ish had made offers to buy us, but that his father always refused to part with us. More than once, after a visit from Wic-an-an-ish, Maquinna had said to me, "John. You no run 'way?"

"Run away, Maquinna? No."

"If you make run 'way, John, I kill."

"We shall not run away, Maquinna."

"That is good."

All this was going through my mind as we followed Sat-sat down the forested mountain toward the village at its foot. I watched for clearings in the trees, trying to get a glimpse of the Indian houses on the grassy plain below.

We stumbled on, with Jack at our heels. Sat-sat hurried ahead. It was a chance for Sails and myself to exchange a word or two.

"What do you make of it, Sails?" I asked.

"I reckon it's a bit suspicious, lad. There's a squall blowing up, if you ask me. But there's no running away from it, I reckon. Better stow all sail and ride it out. What do you say, lad?"

I agreed.

We were in a somewhat breathless state by the time we entered the village. There were signs of a recent salmon feast: dying fires, and roasting-sticks lying about. All was quiet, and the inhabitants within doors. We saw the magnificent canoes of the visitors. Two Wic-an-an-ish Indians stood guard beside them. Dusk was falling, and a gentle snow descending. The lamps had been lit in Maquinna's house. We followed Sat-sat in.

Inside, it reminded me, at first, of a congregation in a church. Wic-an-an-ish and his people sat together on one side; Maquinna and his people on the other. They faced each other across the middle space. But as we entered, all eyes turned to look at us.

Maquinna beckoned us to sit on the bench at his side, facing the visitors. I thought he looked uneasy, as did the under-chiefs around him. The women offered us food, but we declined it.

"John—Tom-soon," Maquinna said slowly, in his deep rolling voice. "Wic-an-an-ish bring news from coast. Much talk of ships. White men's ships."

"Ships at Nootka, Tyee?" I asked, with undisguised excitement.

"Ships not at Nootka, John. *Talk* of ships. Talk of soon. Soon they come."

"Oh, now I see what you mean, Squire," said Sails. "There's a rumor spreading on the coast that some trading ships are on their way. I never seen such a place for rumors as this coast. Due to arrive this spring, as usual, are they? Well, good; let 'em all come, say I; the more the merrier."

While Sails was having his say, thoughts were buzzing

through my head. Ships—coming to Nootka—then we would be rescued. It was wonderful news. And then, as if to temper my enthusiasm, the sober thought entered my head that this might all be a trick. It might be Wic-an-an-ish tricking Maquinna. Or, again, it might be the result of a growing rumor—a rumor started by Sails himself, since he lost no opportunity, whenever he was out of sorts, of declaring to everybody that a fleet of white men's ships would come to Nootka one day and give them *what for*.

"Now let's get this straight," Sails was saying, and because he wanted Maquinna to understand him, he slowed up, and spoke more clearly. "Ships, you say, Squire? Ships."

"Ships," repeated Maquinna.

"Coming to Nootka?"

"To Nootka, yes."

"And soon, eh?"

"Soon. Yes."

"Any idea how many, Squire? How many? Two? Three?"

"Twenty," said Maquinna. "Talk of twenty."

"*Twenty!*" bellowed Sails in amazement.

"*Twenty!*" I cried out at the same time. "Why that's a whole fleet, Maquinna."

"That's a lot of ships, Squire, to come to Nootka for trade."

"No trade!" Maquinna raised his voice. "War. Come to kill."

I gave Sails a quick glance. I was all hot inside. I searched my shipmate's countenance for some clue. His large face was a complete blank. But I thought I saw a quick flicker of movement in one of his eyes—the very slightest evidence of a wink.

Wic-an-an-ish was now speaking to Maquinna from across the space. I strained to get his meaning. It seemed that he was making a demand: that we should each in turn get up and speak, and that the outcome would depend on whether we gave a good account of ourselves. Maquinna was at first reluctant to allow it, but Wic-an-an-ish insisted in his demands, raising his voice and his arms as he did so. At last, Maquinna turned to me.

"John. You speak," he said.

"But what shall I say?" I was in no state of mind to make a speech to Wic-an-an-ish.

"Tell about white men. Why they come. What we do."

I stood up. My heart was beating fiercely. Perhaps our lives were at stake, and depended on what I was now about to say. I faced Wic-an-an-ish and I spoke.

"Red men," I said, "this is your country—your home. I am white man. Tom-soon is white man. We are your guests. You feed us. You let us live among you. But many moons away, across a great ocean, is the home of white men: my home; the home of Tom-soon also. We are what you call King George Men."

"*Kintshaushmen*," they cried in chorus. "We know."

"But our ship belonged to Boston Men," I said. "And the Boston Men live in your country, which is very, very large, stretching far over these mountains. One day white men will come over these mountains from the East, and you will say, 'We are all brothers because we live in the same big country.'

"It is true. Red men and white men are brothers. We must live at peace. White men want furs. Red men want iron and copper. If many ships come to Nootka, they bring much iron and copper. It is good that the white men come. They come to trade. If there are many ships, there will be much trade. I say it is good."

I sat down.

"It is good," said Maquinna. He turned to Sails.

"Tom-soon speak," he said.

My shipmate took from his mouth the piece of sedge grass which he had been holding between his teeth ever since our arrival in the village. Then he glanced toward the entrance. The snow was still falling lightly outside, and filtering into the house. The sky between the roof planks was black and heavy. Sails looked toward Maquinna and nodded. He didn't bother to stand up; and he bellowed out his words.

"The lad's right," he said. "The lad's right. Plenty trade. Plenty. And that's where we can help you Indians —us two. This blacksmith here, and me; both of us can help you. We can speak well of you to the ships' Captains. We can give you written recommends to take aboard and show the Captain—letters saying good of you—because this lad can write. He can *write*, I say. That's more than any of you can do. It's more than I can do. We never went to school, you and me. But this lad did. And he can write letters for the Captains to read. He's written some already."

He took out a bundle of the letters from a secret pocket in his jacket, and waved them in the air. I was amazed at his boldness. But there was no stopping him now. "Here, pass 'em round," he said. "Take a look at 'em. Give your eyes a treat."

Already the paper leaves were moving from hand to hand and keen eyes were peering at them.

Meanwhile a change came over the assembled Indians. Conviviality broke out among them. Fires blazed up. The blackness of the night outside was forgotten. The floating feathers of snow coming in through the gaps danced like moths beside the burning lamps, and died of jollity. Scowls of resentment disappeared. Feasting began; and song; and Sat-sat's wolf dance.

Then Maquinna asked me to sing to the visitors, as I had done a year ago at Tashees, in that very house, with the night outside dark and the forest quiet. So I sang Christmas hymns and ballads of old England, long into the night; and Sails gave a fair representation of a sailor's hornpipe. From time to time we ate broiled salmon, followed by pressed berries and whale oil for cream.

At last, weariness fell upon all. I was dog-tired, and so was Sails. He told Wic-an-an-ish he could keep a couple of letters; the rest he gathered in, some of them much the worse for wear.

We went to our benches. I must have fallen asleep instantly. How long I slept, I do not know. But what I *do* know, and am not likely to forget, was the shock of being awakened by a terrific clap of thunder. I know that it set my heart pounding like a sledgehammer, and that I cried out in alarm and leaped from my sleeping bench at the shock. Another peal, even heavier, followed a flash of lightning which turned night into momentary day. I ran to the entrance and peered out. Snow was still falling. I remember my amazement at this: to have snow, and thunder and lightning at one and the same time.

Well, there I stood, dazed, looking out, and feeling an unusual dullness and heaviness in my head. Behind me, I was vaguely aware of people moving about, disturbed like me by the sudden alarm. Another lightning flash lit up the whole exterior, so that I could see the houses, and the trees, and the black stretch of water outside, on which the canoes of Wic-an-an-ish had looked so imposing. But the next flash revealed that those canoes had disappeared.

I turned to wake up Sails and tell him. In the dimness of the house, I was stumbling to his bench. I bent down, intending to shake him by the shoulder to wake him. But his bench was forsaken. My shipmate was gone.

"Sails—where are you?" I cried, in sudden panic. My head was suddenly dizzy. I remember putting my hand to my forehead, to find it damp, feverish and hot. I remember my knees going suddenly weak. I remember somehow dragging my heavy body to my own bench, on which I must have fallen. And after that, consciousness swam away from me, and I knew no more.

17

Fever

How many hours went by after I had collapsed upon my bed, I do not know. When I opened my eyes, broad daylight was spilling through the gaps and fissures of the building. My eyelids were painfully heavy, my eyes themselves hurting with stabs of pain; and my head ached and thumped dreadfully. My limbs were so heavy with weariness that I felt no wish to move them, but only to let them lie still.

My bed seemed somehow different; the blankets were new and clean. Then I became aware of an Indian girl sitting at my bedside. She was cooling my brow with snow from a large shell. I looked at her, and she smiled.

"John's head has much fire," she said.

I tried to nod, to show that I understood; and to smile, to show that I was grateful to her.

Then the dread happenings of the night came back to

me: the thunderstorm, the canoes gone, and my shipmate missing. I sat up and cried out, "Where—where is Sails?"

I turned my head this way and that, trying to search the dark interior with my eyes for any sign of my shipmate. But everything was blurred and indefinite. I was aware of a few figures lurking in the shadows. At my shouts, they looked up for a moment, then turned to their pursuits again. Exhausted, I fell back heavily upon the bed, and closed my eyes.

And with my eyes tightly closed, I began feverishly to see, or to dream again, that nightmarish affair back at Nootka, when Sails had killed the Wic-an-an-ish Indian. I saw again that shocking scene—Sails washing the blankets and spreading them on the grass to dry in the sun. The Indian deliberately stepping on them, walking all over them, dirtying them. Over and over again, he did so, heedless of warnings. And then I saw Sails, in his rage, taking a cutlass and, with one blow, striking the Indian's head from his body.

This scene was so firmly imprinted on my mind, that it became more vivid and horrible every time I recalled it. But now, in my feverish nightmare, that severed head upon the ground began to speak, and to warn my shipmate that the Wic-an-an-ish Indians would have revenge on him. At this, I cried out in my delirium.

Then, I opened my eyes, and the terrible nightmare was gone. I was still in bed, in Maquinna's longhouse at Tashees; and the gentle Indian girl was cooling my head with snow. And after a little while, I sank into a deep sleep.

When I next awoke, I remember feeling warm and comfortable. The girl was still sitting beside my bed. It was dark; but I could see that she was still smiling. For all I knew, she might have been sitting like that for days, and smiling all the time. I recognized her for a niece of Maquinna; gentle, never raising her voice much above a whisper. She leaned toward me, and spoke.

"Tom-soon, he is here," she said. Then again, after a pause, "Tom-soon is here. He sleeps."

With a deep sigh of relief, I accepted her word without question. I smiled at her in the dimness, allowed my head to sink into the pillow of blankets, and closed my eyes to sleep again.

And the next time I awoke, Sails was indeed there beside me, his large face bending over me. I sat up, and reached out and touched his face.

"Sails, you're here! Where have you been? Tell me where you've been," I demanded.

"Never you mind where I've been," he replied. "I'm back now. You get yourself better; then I'll tell you."

"But, Sails, I must know—now. I found your bed empty, and the canoes gone. I thought they'd carried you off with them."

"You thought right, lad. Carried me off in my sleep, like an innocent babe. But I gave 'em the slip."

"You did? Where?"

"About ten miles down; when they pulled into a creek for a bit of shut-eye. That's when I daddled 'em. Nipped into the forest; forgot all about my rheumatism; and found my way back here."

"And Maquinna? What did he say?"

A change came over my shipmate's face. It was like the sun going behind a cloud. I could see that Sails suspected something—suspected that Maquinna had played some part in his capture.

"I wish I knew," he said, almost as though he were thinking aloud. "I only wish I knew." Then, more loudly, he continued, "Maquinna says there'll be war with Wic-an-an-ish. We're leaving for Cooptee any day now. Cooptee's more open. You can see who's coming at Cooptee. So you get yourself better."

And then the sun came from behind the cloud again, and his face brightened as he said, "And see who's coming now—your little Indian lily. She saved your life, I reckon. A nasty fever and chill, that's what you had."

The Indian girl came toward me, shyly, and washed my hands and face as if I were a child.

A few days later, we moved downstream to Cooptee, where Maquinna made me eat many herrings to regain my strength.

The year before at Cooptee Maquinna had urged us to dress and live like his own people. I thought I knew why. Looking like Indians, we could not be recognized for the white men we were—by other Indians who might wish to carry us off. Nor could we be noticed by our own people, should they suddenly put in an appearance with a trading ship.

If Maquinna was silent now on this particular matter, he was more than ready to speak on two others. The first took me completely off my guard.

"John," he said, "you live with us always—you take wife."

"But . . ." I stammered, completely taken aback. My thoughts were on escape, not on settling with the Indians for the rest of my life. However, it seemed prudent to keep these thoughts to myself.

"John," said Maquinna again, after a pause.

"Yes, Tyee?"

"At Nootka, we hunt *Mah-hak*."

"Yes, Tyee, I know. You will begin to hunt the whale as soon as we return to Nootka. And you, Tyee, because you are Tyee, must hurl the first harpoon and take the first blood, out in the ocean. It is the custom of your tribe."

Maquinna turned to look behind him, and pointed to the snow-capped mountain which stood clear-cut against a beautiful clear blue sky. "You see, John?"

"Yes, Tyee, I see the mountain."

"Tomorrow, John, I go there—to think of whales."

"I know, Tyee. I understand. You will go alone to meditate—to pray for success at the whale hunt."

"John—tell me about white man's harpoon."

"The white man's harpoon is strong," I said. "It is made of iron."

"John make me harpoon—yes?"

"Yes, Tyee, I will make you harpoons of iron. I will build a forge of brick and rock at Nootka. I will build it on the beach. Then I will make charcoal in the forest. And when that is done, I will smelt some bar iron; and with a large rock for anvil and my hammer from the ship, I will fashion you a harpoon such as the white men use."

Maquinna nodded. His face brightened ever so slightly, which was a most unusual thing. Anyone could tell that Tyee Maquinna was a worried man. He had the Wic-an-an-ish Indians and their tricks to worry about; and also he worried about his prowess at whaling. In the last whaling season, when the whales migrated up the coast and swam and spouted off Nootka, he had had no success. In the coming season, everything depended on his being successful—or he could be deposed in favor of a younger chief. And if that happened, of course, the lives of Sails and myself would not be worth a farthing.

"Yes, Tyee," I said eagerly, "I will make you harpoons of iron; harpoons that will be strong and sure. I will also make you blubber spades and lances; and Tom-soon will make you whaling lines and fasten them securely on the harpoons."

"It is good," said Maquinna. "It is good."

Every day for a whole week Maquinna left the village

and climbed the mountain which overshadowed us. He went alone, to pray for success in his whale-hunting; because he was Maquinna, the whale-killer, he, and he alone, must strike the first whale, or give way to a younger man. I felt truly sorry for him. Early every morning, I watched him go. All day, my thoughts were with him. Every evening, I watched for his return; and he would say:

"John, you make me harpoon?"

"Yes, Tyee Maquinna. I have already promised."

"Make me strong harpoon."

"I will make you harpoons of iron, Tyee."

"Make me harpoons such as the white men use."

"Yes, Tyee. I have already promised. I will forge you harpoons, strong and sure, such as the white men use."

During the following week, we were kept very busy. My shipmate made a sail for Maquinna's canoe; I made him a blubber spade out of sheet metal, with a strong wooden handle, and demonstrated to him how it might be used on a captured whale. Together, we overhauled our longboat, making it shipshape and seaworthy.

And on February 19, 1805, according to the reckoning in my journal—a fine, clear, sunny day—we dismantled our houses, loaded the canoes, and set out for Nootka and the sea once more.

18

Sat-sat Throws a Harpoon

Nothing at Nootka had changed, except that grass had begun to grow again on the clearing, and the village had a fresher, spring-cleaned look.

The next morning we all set to work at daybreak to assemble the houses; they were finished and ready for habitation by nightfall. During the day, strangers came with presents of wild geese.

"Tomorrow," said Sat-sat, "we have feast of wild geese."

"Good," I said. "I shall invite you to eat roast goose with Tom-soon and me. Tom-soon very good cook."

Sat-sat was looking at my feet. They were cut and sore because Maquinna forbade us anymore to wear the rope shoes that Sails made for us. "*Peshak*," Sat-sat said.

"Yes, very *peshak*," I agreed. "Your father says his under-chiefs insist that we must look like Indians and go barefoot; but I am a white man, and white men wear shoes. Without shoes, my feet are *peshak*. And Tomsoon has rheumatism—much fire in him. Also we have no more soap. With soap I could clean the sores of my feet."

"Poor John," he said. "You not very good Indian. In ten moons—twenty moons—thirty moons—forty moons, you very good red man. You live with us always—take wife—hunt *mah-hak*—become great chief."

I shook my head.

"Yes, yes," he insisted. "Tomorrow you make harpoons to hunt *mah-hak?*"

"Yes," I said. "Tomorrow I want you to help me to build a forge near the water. Together we will make charcoal for the forge. Then, with some bar iron, and a stone for an anvil we will forge an iron harpoon such as the white men use."

"John—you show me how use harpoon?"

"Yes, if you wish."

"I wish."

"All right. We'll go out in a canoe in the Sound and you shall practice using the white man's harpoon."

"It is good. My father say it is good."

Preparations for the whaling now began in earnest. We built our forge on the beach, and set ourselves up as a manufactory of whaling gear: harpoons, lances, spades and blubber knives. Then, for several days together, Maquinna went out of the house alone, early in the morning, to pray to his god Quahootzee, the Great Tyee of the Sky. In token of humiliation, he bound a broad band of

129

red bark around his head, with a green twig of spruce fastened to it like a crest. Day after day, he left the longhouse without a word to anyone, and disappeared into the woods.

During his absence, the strongest and most virile whaling men of the village began their own preparations. Several times a day, they ran headlong into the cold sea to bathe, after which they scoured their bodies with sharp-edged shells and rough twigs till the blood flowed. And this toughening process went on for two whole weeks. I asked Sat-sat why they chastized themselves in this manner; and he told me.

"To catch a whale is not easy," he said. "Whale very big—man very small. Man must have help of spirit to catch whale."

"And how does a man get the help of a spirit, Sat-sat?"

"I tell you. Listen. Man beat himself with sticks; man stay long time in water, doing like whale." Here, Sat-sat pretended to be a whale in the water, plunging, turning and twisting, diving, and coming up to spout.

"Also man go without food; man go without food for three days," Sat-sat continued.

"But how does that bring him spirit help?"

"I tell you. Listen. Spirit see him. Spirit watch him. Spirit say, 'That man very brave—I help him.'"

"And what sort of spirit is it that helps him?"

"Maybe spirit of wolf. Wolves great hunters. Maybe spirit of seabird; seabirds follow whale. Maybe the great whale himself—*Mah-hak*."

"And how exactly does the spirit help the man to be a whale hunter?" I asked.

"Spirit teach him songs; songs to bring whale alongside canoe; songs to make whale happy; songs to bring whale home."

Sat-sat immediately began to chant, in a low, haunting key:

Whale, come alongside my canoe;
When I spear you, do not be afraid;
Harpoon, when I throw you, take fast hold;
Whale, if I miss, take my harpoon in your hands;
Whale, do not break my canoe.

"My father teach me much about *Mah-hak*," Sat-sat said. "This time, I think my father let me go in canoe. One day, I take my father's place in canoe. I am not boy. I am man. I am brave. I have spirit help from wolf."

"I know you are brave, Sat-sat. When I came to Nootka you were boy. Now you are almost man. I also am man; though when I came to Nootka I felt very young—like a boy. Tom-soon still treats me as if I were a boy; but like you, I have grown up."

"John many moons at Nootka," said Sat-sat.

"Twenty-six moons," I said.

We were sitting on the beach, looking out across the Sound toward the sea.

"Whale sing too," Sat-sat went on.

"What does the whale sing, Sat-sat?"

"I tell you. Listen." And Sat-sat began a new song, deep and guttural, from the back of his throat:

131

Here I come;
　　Come from the ocean;
　　　Come to the land;
　　　　To visit many people.

Here I come;
　　To be caught again.

We got to our feet, and returned to the forge. "Sat-sat," I said, "I will make a harpoon for you. I will make the spearhead of sharpened steel, to replace the mussel shell. It will be a mussel shell made out of steel; and this can be fixed, like your mussel shells, to the pincers of elk-horn. It will not be heavy. For Tyee Maquinna, I will make harpoons like the white men's harpoons; but they will be heavy."

"It is good," said Sat-sat. "It is good. My father say so."

For the next few days, I worked at my forge in the mornings, and went out in a canoe with Sat-sat in the afternoons. Meanwhile, the women and children were kept busy, making lines of whale sinew, deer sinew, and twisted roots of spruce and cedar. The lines were of different thicknesses. Some of the men were preparing sealskin bladders to be used as floats, to fasten to the lines. Sails sat apart, unraveling some canvas to make thread, his dog curled up beside him.

On several afternoons, when the weather was not too blustery, Sat-sat and I took out a medium-sized canoe, and paddled it a little way up the Sound, Sat-sat at the prow, myself in the stern, both of us plying our paddles.

Then, in a suitable place, we dropped a bundle of sea-weed to float on the water. This, we pretended, was a whale. We approached it from every side, myself pad-dling, steering, and bringing the canoe to within a few feet of the mock whale on the larboard side. Sat-sat stood at the prow, the harpoon in his hand, with one foot hooked around a thwart for safety. Each time we ap-proached the floating weed, at six to ten feet from it, I called out, "Now—*throw!*"

Sat-sat hurled the harpoon, fastened as it was to about fifty feet of line. This line was tied to the prow of the canoe, so that we could haul the harpoon back, and coil the line, ready for another throw. The shaft of supple cedarwood, which was made to fall away from the har-poon head, we could usually pick up, though we had some spares in case of loss.

With every throw, I approached the floating seaweed a little less closely, so that Sat-sat was obliged to hurl his harpoon with increasing vigor. At last he would be tired and ready for home. He coiled the line at the prow, rested his harpoon in the notch specially made for it, and took up his paddle. There was a ripple on the surface of the water, which produced millions of dazzling cold dia-monds of light whenever the sun escaped from behind white scudding clouds.

On one occasion we were about halfway back to Friendly Cove, when I saw through the dazzle of sun-shine what appeared to be a little cloud of thin smoke close to the surface of the water, and not a dozen yards away. Then our canoe began to rock and shake, and instantly I knew what was causing it. A whale was indeed surfacing close by. At once, Sat-sat was on the alert; and the next moment, the real whale had passed our canoe, within ten feet of us. It was not a large one; I could see its shape distinctly below the water; and in that second of time, while I was keeping the canoe in balance against the swell and wash of water, I heard myself shouting in a shrill, excited voice: "Now—*throw!*"

Sat-sat was on his feet in the prow. His body stiffened. He had not reached for the harpoon. He seemed to be covering his face with a hand. Then, as the whale disappeared, he turned on me a look of reproach.

"No. *Not* throw!" he said; then turned to pick up his paddle and proceed. And then I understood my foolishness. I had unwittingly tried to make him break a solemn custom of his tribe—the unwritten law which decreed that the head chief of the tribe—the Tyee himself—should strike the first whale. Sat-sat neither spoke nor looked at me during the rest of our journey back. Nor did he ever go out with me again to practice harpooning.

19

The Great Forbearance

The weeks went by. May came, and June, with an occasional whale in the Sound, and Indians watching out for them from vantage points along the rocky cliffs. Maquinna's whaling men put themselves into a state of readiness.

Maquinna's whaling canoe was forty feet long, with a prow like a viking ship. It was painted red on the inside and charred black on the outside. Five thwarts, or crosspieces, divided the canoe into sections, from stem to stern. These crosspieces were covered with bark mats, and under these were kept the items of whaling gear. Bark and sinew ropes were coiled in the bow, where the harpoons rested in their notches. These were the harpoons made by me of sharpened steel. When ready for use, they were attached to ropes and to a detachable shaft. These harpoons were, in fact, a combination of the hunter's spear and the fisherman's hook and line. When the shaft fell away, the rope and hook remained secure. Wooden scoops (for baling out water) and six sealskin floats (not yet inflated) were stored away.

At last all was ready.

Morning came, with a clear sun; out in the Sound, foam flecks broke against rocks and headlands. Farther out, we could see, by dint of peering and concentrating our gaze, the vague shapes of the bulky creatures, raising a tail fluke out of the water before diving in a swirl of ocean.

In the village, as the sun came up across the Sound, all was suddenly bustle and excitement. Maquinna's crew of whalers, scoured and toughened by their exercises of the past weeks, left the house, each carrying his paddle. They reached the beach, floated the canoe, jumped lightly aboard, and struck out, with smooth, rapid strokes, toward the ocean. Other canoes followed, keeping their distance; and women and children ran into the water, saying prayers for success, and waving good luck.

"Come, Sails," I said, catching at the general excitement. I set off to run to the headland on the south side of the Cove, in the same way that, at home, I might have set off at a run to follow the fox hunters.

"What's the hurry, lad?" Sails grumbled, as he stumbled after me. His dog followed at his heels.

Maquinna's canoe, leading, turned the headland and left the Cove, disappearing, for the time being, out of sight. As it vanished behind the cliffs, I saw Maquinna at the prow, alert, with the harpoon already in his grasp. He was looking proudly and defiantly ahead. None could strike a whale until *he* had done so; that was the law of his tribe.

We ran on, panting for breath, toward the headland from where we could watch the grim sport, the outcome of which was so vital to Maquinna. His power and position depended now on his ability, or his luck, to bring in a whale. If he failed—I thought—Nootka would have another Tyee, after which the fate of Sails and myself didn't bear thinking about.

We sat upon the headland, where the cliff descended almost vertically to the sea below, and there, recovering our breath, we strained our eyes to catch it all. The sun was bright and glittering; we had to shade our eyes against it. I wished I had the ship's telescope; but it was with Maquinna in the canoe. I prayed it might help him now.

At last, we saw a whale surfacing not far from Maquinna's canoe. It spouted, dived, and struck the water with an upraised fluke. Other whales appeared. They seemed now to be aware of their pursuers, and to be moving farther out to sea. The canoes were streaking after them.

Then I saw Maquinna's arm uplifted; the thrown harpoon flashed in the sunlight; I held my breath and hoped that he had struck. The next moment I saw one of the following canoes upturned; and we heard the faint startled cry as the occupants fell and dived into the sea, or, it may be, on the very back of the whale that had spun around to upset them. The men were splashing in the water, making for nearby canoes and scrambling aboard, while their own canoe, quickly filling with water, suddenly went nose under, and sank.

By this time, Maquinna had pulled back the ineffective harpoon, and his canoe sailed in pursuit, out of the Sound, and out of our vision.

We sat, for a while, in silence. My shipmate chewed a piece of coarse grass between his stained teeth. Then he spat.

"They won't strike a whale, not they," he muttered in disgust. "And serve 'em right, if they haven't the sense to use a proper harpoon, after you sweats at the forge making 'em."

I was puzzled. "But they *are* using my harpoons," I said.

"No," he said. "They're not."

"But I saw my harpoons stowed at the prow of the canoe."

"So you did, lad. But I'll tell you what you *didn't* see. You didn't see 'em take your harpoons out of the canoe, first thing this morning, and put Indian mussel shell harpoons in their place."

"You're joking, Sails."

"I'm not," he replied, flatly.

At that moment, Sat-sat ran up to us, with other Indian boys at his heels. They chattered with excitement.

"You saw my father throw harpoon, John?" he asked.

"Yes," I said.

"He missed," said Sails.

"Sat-sat, is it true—" I asked him "—is it true that Tyee Maquinna has not taken the harpoons I made for him?"

"It is true," said Sat-sat.

"But why?" I asked.

"Men say white men's harpoons not good. Bring mischief. My father very angry: say John's harpoons good. Men say no: John's harpoons *peshak*. Men say use red men's harpoons in red man's country."

"I see," I said, feeling more disappointed than angry. I had hoped Maquinna would have success with the harpoons I had made him. But now I found myself hoping that an Indian mussel shell would bring him quicker success. It certainly was lighter in weight than a white man's iron harpoon, and in consequence easier for an Indian to use. And it was the weapon that the Indians had themselves devised, as being most suitable to their needs.

Meanwhile my shipmate was saying, with the finality of an oracle, "They'll catch no whales. You'll see. And serve 'em right."

And he was right.

As the dusky sunset began to color the cold sea, the weary and disgruntled whalers returned to shore, and disappeared into their houses. Maquinna spoke to no one, but solemnly departed from his house to spend the night alone in the forest.

In the morning he returned. The Nootka whalers followed him to the beach again, and into their canoes and away. He needed no scouts to watch for whales now. Somewhere down the Sound and out at sea whales could certainly be found, and Maquinna was determined to find them. He was desperate. One had to admire his courage.

But again he had no success; and yet again the following day; and the day after that. Maquinna and his men returned each evening, tired, frustrated and angry, and disappeared into their houses. The evenings were silent and deserted, save for the screeches of the nighthawks flying through the sky overhead. Maquinna either visited the forest or the cliffs along the Sound to pray, or he remained silent and morose in his compartment of the house, with Sails and myself nearby.

"Why don't you use a proper harpoon, Squire?" said my shipmate, with a show of impatience. "We've made a supply for you. They're ready, with barbs ground and sharpened. You could take 'em tomorrow. Trouble is, your men needs a bit of hazing. You've only to say the word and I'll haze 'em for you. I'll use a paddle, *oo-wha-pa*, on their thick skulls. I'll knock a bit of sense into their thick heads. You just say the word, Squire."

This spirited outburst sounded more like the old Sails, before the recent onset of rheumatics. It cheered me up, I must confess, to listen to some of his old banter. But what Maquinna made of the speech, it is hard to say. He looked puzzled, and at the same time heartened. But if he understood the offer, he did not accept it. Clearly there was a rigid ritual about Nootka whaling, handed down through the ages. White men could not understand this ritual; they must not interfere. But Maquinna, I felt sure, was at his wit's end to know what to do. After a long silence, he raised his head and spoke to us, quietly.

"John, Tom-soon—you go," he said.

"Go? Go where?" cut in Sails sharply.

Maquinna signed to him to be silent, and to listen; then he continued. "Go into forest. Sleep in forest. Pray in forest. Stay in forest all night. When sun wakes up—come back sure."

Sails was on the point of remonstrating again, but Maquinna raised a finger to his lips for silence.

As we walked away from the house, Indians watched us; and when, some way off, I turned to look at the village, I saw under-chiefs already moving toward Maquinna's house, as though ordered by him to do so.

It was a fine summer night in the forest. We found a mossy bank, and there reclined, discussing the meaning of our expulsion. Sails, after complaining about his rheumatism and the heartlessness of uncivilized varmints, fell quickly asleep. For myself, though I dozed a little, I lay for the most part awake, watching for the sky above the trees to turn from dark violet to the watery pink and blue of dawn.

At first light, we returned to the village. All the Indians were astir. Maquinna was waiting for us. His manner was quite changed. His bearing was prouder than ever. In whatever angry disputation he might have taken part during the night, it was obvious that he had won his way.

"Today, you come in canoe," he said. "We take white man's harpoon."

We were both as excited as schoolboys; and almost before we realized it, we were skimming through the water, with the other canoes close at heel. One of my harpoons was already at the prow, spliced to a rope and resting in a notch. Maquinna passed some dried fish to us. We ate in silence, and drank fresh water from a container filled at the stream. Soon we were out of the Cove, beyond the headland and out in the Sound, making for open sea; and some hours later, we had spotted whales spouting in the distance.

"Thar she blows!" bellowed my shipmate. His cry startled the Indians so much that they caught crabs with their paddles and turned to eye him with disfavor. This sudden breaking of silence seemed to offend them, like crying out in church.

"Now, steady, steady," he said firmly. "*Oo-wha-pa, wik, wik*. Ship your paddles."

Some did not obey at once, but he gave these rebels such a stare and a scowl that they thought better of it and obeyed his order. Maquinna himself readily acquiesced, just as though it were natural for him to take and not to give commands. Then, with a motion of his raised hands, Sails brought the following canoes to a standstill, shaking his fist at the tardy ones.

"Stop—and stay still," he ordered, "and sooner or later we'll have a whale on our bows; but you've got to keep still, and wait. You've got to have great patience, I'm telling you. It'll pay you in the end."

For a long time we drifted thus.

And then, at last, our great forbearance was rewarded. Out of the dusk and silence, there came a sound, the sound of an approaching whale. It had risen to spout not ten yards away. Water lapped against the canoe, making it sway. Maquinna grasped the harpoon.

"Wait!" breathed Sails, raising a forbidding hand.

Maquinna waited.

Then the enormous gray bulk of the mammal was at our very side. Maquinna threw the harpoon with all his force. The canoe swayed dangerously. Then, hearing a cry, I saw that Maquinna had lost his balance. He tried to right himself, but the swaying canoe went against him, and with arms spread and hands clutching at the empty air, he stumbled and fell overboard. At the same time, the waters around us seemed to open up. A huge whale fluke, like a dark cloud, hovered above us, then thrashed down on the water and was gone. This action threw Maquinna upward, and I saw his struggling body come down on the starboard side, within a few feet of where Sails was kneeling on a thwart.

"Grab my legs, lad," he shouted to me, as he shot out an arm, and clutched Maquinna by the hair. The canoe rocked. The Indians shouted. I grabbed hold of Sails.

"Trim the canoe, you swabs, or we'll all be overboard," shouted Sails. They didn't understand him, but they knew what to do. It all happened in a second. The whale was taking out the line, to which were attached sealskin floats to act as brakes and to keep the whale at the surface. And at the same time, Maquinna was being hauled aboard, dripping water from every part of his body—from his hair, his ears and his wide-open mouth. And this was only just in time; for now the line was paid out, and the whale was taking the canoe for a ride.

The other canoes were all about us. Lances and javelins were flying through the shadowy air. The Indians were shouting and shrieking in a confused tumult of sound and fury. And now we were moving, faster and faster through the water, and on, and on, and on. The line was taut and straining; the harpoon had struck home, and had held.

For how long or how far we went thus, I do not know, but at length our canoe was motionless again. Paddles were grasped; the canoe sped forward; the line was coiled in: until, among a sea of floating inflated sealskins we came upon our prize.

I shall never forget the excitement of the Indians, nor the look of relief on Maquinna's face.

"*Wau-kash*," he said. "It is good."

Very quickly, the other canoes made fast with their lines to the whale's carcass to tow it back to Nootka. It was a long way, but nobody minded that. And long before we had touched the beach at Friendly Cove, my tired, old, and triumphant shipmate had dropped his head upon his chest, and fallen into a sound sleep.

As the dawn light crept over the village of Nootka, we sailed in with our capture, singing our success in a melodious chant to the rhythm of the paddle strokes. The villagers were awaiting us. All night they had kept vigil on the rooftops. They drummed and beat upon the houses, and shouted their welcome in chorus.

"*Wau-kash! Wau-kash! Wau-kash!*"

Throughout the day, the Indians cut up the whale blubber, while the whalers rested; and at night we had a feast. Maquinna, apparently no worse for his adventure, presided over the feast and made an oration, in which he praised the good sense and the steady arm of Tom-soon, whose very name was a promise of good fortune.

Then he spoke of his own great wish, as the Tyee of his tribe. It was his wish, he said, soon, to hand over the leadership of his whaling canoe to Sat-sat-sok-sis, his son. The boy was not yet ready, he said. He had not yet the strength nor the skill. But, because he was a boy, he would learn: and with the help of Tom-soon, he would learn quickly. He, Maquinna, head of the Nootka tribe, would ask John and Tom-soon, during the coming weeks, to teach the boy the great patience, out in the ocean, waiting for the whale: so that in a year's time, Sat-sat-sok-sis would succeed him at the prow of the canoe, where he, Maquinna, the whale hunter, had held command for so much of his long life.

20

A Ship in the Offing

Next day the whaling men rested. The others continued to dispose of the whale's carcass. Meanwhile, all who had taken part in the capture were given their share of blubber to boil. What remained after the oil had been extracted tasted rather like pork. Meanwhile, Sails went with his dog up to the headland to look out to sea.

Sat-sat came up to me and said, "Today, John go with me to see *Quart-lak*."

"I'm agreeable," I said. "How do we go?"

"In my canoe."

"And where do we go?"

Sat-sat pointed across the Sound to an island where I knew that, under the rocky cliffs, in the kelp beds, sea otter were sometimes to be found.

"You go to hunt *Quart-lak?*" I asked.

"No," he replied.

"Good," I said. The hunting of that delightful creature, the sea otter, was something I was determined never to engage in. I had already seen these animals (while quietly peering from above them) lying on their backs in the kelp, floating or eating or sleeping, or playing with their young. I had also seen hunters, working in pairs, using arrows and spears to kill or wound them. I had seen beaches strewn with carcasses, and the sand stained with blood. And so I was glad to go with Sat-sat to watch, but not to kill them. We had floated the canoe, and were about to depart, when Maquinna came up.

"I go with you," he said.

We took a larger canoe and pushed off. Tyee Maquinna was also glad to leave his duties for a while. He had shown a sense of high responsibility and resolve. He had done what custom had demanded of him. He had struck the first whale. Now he could leave the arduous business to others.

We crossed the Sound to the rocky islands and the kelp beds where the sea otter abounded. We passed the cove where Captain Cook had first anchored the *Resolution*, before visiting Nootka village; and I thought of the great man again. I could always take heart—even in my most dismal moments—by recalling the great navigator, and by reminding myself that I was treading ground that he had trod, and sailing in waters where he had sailed.

"Tyee—did Captain Cook watch the sea otter?" I asked.

"Yes. Captain Cook go with me in canoe. Like now."

"Did Captain Cook hunt the sea otter?"

"No. Him watch."

"Did he ever shoot them?"

"No. Not shoot. Captain Cook not carry musket. Him good man. In my house many times. Always my friend. John, tell me . . . Captain Cook come back?"

This question surprised me. "Why, Tyee," I said, "have I never told you what happened to Captain Cook? Eight moons after he left Nootka, he landed on an island far across this ocean, called Hawaii, and there he met his death. The people of the island killed him; and all his seamen wept."

Maquinna was silent for what seemed a long time. Then, all he said was, "Captain Cook good man." That was all. Sat-sat and I were paddling the canoe. There was a light, fresh breeze on the water.

We reached the kelp beds, and there, resting our paddles, we brought our canoe to a halt between rocks along the shore. We remained silent, watching for sea otter. At first it seemed that they had all disappeared, fled, perhaps, from molesting men. But at length we caught sight of one swimming under water, and saw it surface. It was rather like a seal, except that it had webbed feet and a velvety pelt. It had not noticed us. It lay on its back, floating and sunning itself. After a while it began to crack shells on its chest and to eat the contents.

I was wondering what next it might do, when I found myself turning to look at the distant ocean; and there, to my astonishment, I swear I saw the masts of a ship in full sail, on the point of dropping below the horizon. With great difficulty I suppressed my excitement, and, the more to conceal it, turned toward the otter again. But I was shaking with agitation; and a kind of magnet was pulling my head around to look again at the ship. Unable to resist, I turned. Maquinna and Sat-sat, always on the alert, turned also to follow my gaze. But what they saw was not the ship, but a party in canoes, arriving at Nootka and beginning to beach their craft.

Within seconds, our paddles were in our hands, the sea otter had dived out of sight, and we were streaking across the Sound, back home to Nootka, where Maquinna and Sat-sat jumped ashore. They hurried over to the party of waiting visitors. Among these, I could see Chief Ulatilla, Chief of the Kla-iz-arts. I heard him speak of white men's ships. Maquinna eagerly led the visitors toward his house. For my part, I caught sight of my shipmate waving to me from the headland. The next moment, I was hurrying toward him.

Both Sails and his dog were in a state of great excitement. They ran a few steps to meet me. "Lad, lad, there's a ship out yonder," he cried, as I came up.

"I saw it, Sails," I said, panting for breath.

"I guess it's common news by now, lad."

"Yes. That was Chief Ulatilla who arrived just now. I heard him say he'd been aboard white men's ships, and that they want to trade. Cheer up, Sails. I think our chance has come at last."

"Maybe so, lad," he said. He was shaking as he spoke. "Trouble is, you can't trust these Indians. They're full of tricks. One Chief tricks another. The swabs in this village tries to trick Maquinna. Maquinna tries to trick us. And now the time has come, by Davy Jones, to trick Maquinna; that is, if we plays our cards right."

He grabbed my arm, drew me closer to him, and looked me fiercely in the eye. "Listen to me, lad," he said. "Maquinna wants to trade. He'll risk anything to bring a ship in, and start up trade again. But most of these Indians are scared. They *don't* want a ship to come in. They think it'll bring trouble. They think we shall split on 'em to the ship's captain. We know too much, you and me, about what they did to our ship and our shipmates. They'll want to kill us. Maybe they *will* kill us, unless we can trick 'em. . . . Listen, lad; we've got to trick 'em into thinking that our memories are bad, that we've forgotten what they did to the poor old *Boston*. We've got to trick 'em into thinking that we've lost all interest in white men's ships; that we don't want to go aboard any of 'em. That's the first thing we got to do. It's our only chance, lad."

My shipmate's mind was working fast. From the rheumaticky old man of the past winter, he had suddenly become transformed into a revived and active schemer.

He had been talking with such intensity that we had not noticed what was happening, until the dog growled a warning. Maquinna and the Indians were now congregated on the beach, while Ulatilla himself, alone, was coming in our direction.

"White men's ships," he called, as he approached us. "*Mamethlee, mamethlee!*"

"Keep cool, lad," Sails whispered. "Let him think we ain't much interested."

"John's letter," said Ulatilla, "at last, I have given to white Captain."

"At last!" I said, echoing his words, unable to curb an expression of relief at the news. But Sails was ready for him.

"That letter must have been a bit worn and torn, after all these moons," said Sails coldly. "D'you think the Captain could read it?"

"I go 'board ship—give letter to Captain," said Ulatilla. "You no glad?" He was surprised that we showed no signs of jubilation. He paused for a moment, puzzled, looking first at one of us, then at the other. But without another word, he turned away; and within minutes, his canoes were streaking out of the Cove toward the sea.

During the following days, we worked out our plan of action, or rather my shipmate's plan of action, for, of the two of us, he was the strategist. This stratagem was intended to outwit our enemies, the under-chiefs, who now demanded that we should be instantly killed on the arrival of a ship at Friendly Cove; or, at the very least, that we should be removed into the forest and detained there until the ship had sailed away.

His ruse was not a simple one, but necessity was ever the mother of invention, and Sails had spent many hours devising it. He referred to it as his *Indian Trick*.

The trick was as follows: firstly, we were to spare no pains to implant two notions in the minds of the Indians, viz.: that we had no wish to go aboard a ship; and that by writing a "letter of recommendation" to proffer to the Captain, we could make it safe for Maquinna to do so.

The second part of the plan was to be put into action immediately the ship arrived. We were to persuade Maquinna and a party of his under-chiefs to go aboard, carrying with them the "letter of recommendation" which, in fact, would ask the Captain to put them all in irons till we made good our escape; and this we intended to do by going under cover of trees to a hidden canoe, lying at the water's edge, around an arm of the Cove, while Maquinna was aboard "talking trade." And then, safely on deck, our troubles would be over, Sails said.

"And supposing we are successful in all this, Sails," I inquired, "what will happen to Maquinna?"

"That's for the Captain to decide, lad," he replied.

"I think he should be released," I said.

Sails looked at me rather hard, as at a wavering and doubting conspirator.

"I think he should be released," I said, "on condition that every bit of the *Boston*'s cargo that survives and can be found should be surrendered by the Indians, and put aboard by them."

Sails did not wish to discuss this matter. He made it

clear that his stratagem ended at the point where both of us had set foot on the deck of a rescuing ship.

Inwardly we were at the very peak of excitement; but outwardly we tried hard to appear calm and unconcerned, going about our occupations as we had always done.

And then, at last, on July 19, the day dawned for which we had been waiting so long.

21

The Recommend

I shall never forget that morning. The air was yellow with sunshine, the surf a sparkle of silver. Our cannon-piece on the clearing glinted like gold. We were on the beach. I had finished my morning swim even before the Indians had bestirred themselves. Sails had got the forge going. We glanced down the Sound through the summer haze, in the direction of the Pacific Ocean. And this time we did not look in vain. I caught my shipmate's arm, and gripped it hard. "Sails!" I exclaimed. "Sails . . ."

He straightened his back and looked at me.

"Look out there, Sails! Shade your eyes against the sun."

"My eyes isn't good no more, lad. What is it?"

"Sails, there's a ship in the offing."

I tightened my grip on his arm. His body was trembling.

"I can't see, lad. Me eyes is full of the morning sun; I can't see."

"She's a two-master, Sails; a Boston brig; a trader."

"Is she running in?"

"She's running in."

At that moment, the heartening boom of cannon rumbled across the Cove. My companion's body went rigid, then shook violently. "Cannon; I could see the glint of the guns, lad. It's music to my ears, it is."

I could see that tears were streaming down his large face.

And then the air was full of confused sounds. The birds screeched; the Indians ran out of their houses, turning hither and thither, and pointing out to sea. *"Weena! Weena! Mamethlee!"* they cried. "The white men have come!"

Maquinna came hurrying down to us from his house. Everything would now depend on how we played our cards, as Sails had said. How long had we waited and hoped for this moment! How often had we discussed it, rehearsed it in our minds, worked out what we should do, how we should act!

Maquinna was clearly surprised to find us bent at our work. When he came up, Sails, now to all appearances calm and composed, slowly straightened his back to greet him, and pointed with his arm across the Cove.

"Now's your chance, Squire," he said, "that ship wants to trade with you. That's why she fired off her cannon. Molasses, Maquinna—barrels of the stuff; and blankets, I'll bet, and cloth, and looking glasses, and iron, and copper maybe, and brand-new muskets, like as not."

Maquinna turned to me.

"How John—you no glad go 'board?"

"Don't you go, lad," cut in my shipmate before I had time to get out a reply. I hoped he was not overacting his part. "Take my advice, lad, and keep well to windward of that ship. I know them ship's Captains; they treat you like dogs; tyrants, the lot of 'em. Reckon you and me'll keep out of sight, lad. We'd best go indoors, I reckon. We'll lie low till she sheers off."

Having said this much to me, cunning old fox that he was, he turned to offer further advice to Maquinna.

"Mind you, Squire, there's no reason why *you* shouldn't go aboard. You're a Tyee; you're a King. I reckon nobody would stop King George of England going aboard, if he'd a mind to. You've got sea-otter skins to barter. They've got treacle—loads of it. So what are you waiting for? But as for this lad and me going aboard—no, thank you. We'll be getting out of sight, I reckon. Like as not, the Captain's got a spyglass to his eye this blessed minute. Come on, lad."

To the surprise of Maquinna and his Indians, we made our way toward the longhouse without so much as a second glance at the ship. As we passed our shining cannon-piece, my shipmate halted and called back to Maquinna.

"Hi, Squire; this cannon, here—tell your men to get her out o' sight afore that Captain claps eyes on her."

We entered the deserted longhouse and lurked there in the shadows. Outside, the under-chiefs gathered around Maquinna in a state of considerable agitation. We remained near the door to watch the scene. They were arguing with their Chief, and protesting noisily. I could not doubt that they were demanding our death. Maquinna silenced them. Then he began to speak to them. Catching a word here and there, I guessed that he was proposing to go aboard the brig, but cries of "*Wik, wik*, no, no," showed that they disapproved.

Then I heard him tell his men that he was not afraid of any hurt from the white men on the ship, but that he would be guided by me, because I had always been true to him. He brushed the Indians aside, strode up to his longhouse, and confronted me. "John," he said, looking me full in the face.

"Yes, Tyee Maquinna?"

"You tell me true, John. White men friends?"

My shipmate tried to answer for me, but Maquinna bade him be silent. He wanted an answer from *me*. How could I answer him? Yet answer him, I must.

We were going to play a trick on him. We were going to get him aboard if we possibly could, and have the Captain put him in irons. And now here he was, Tyee Maquinna, asking me, whom he trusted, a simple question that I must answer.

"Tell me true, John—white men friends?"

I answered him evasively. "Certainly, for anything

that I can do, they will treat with you in friendship," I said. "I am sure they will want to barter for your sea-otter furs."

"John write me letter—speak good of me?"

"A recommend," put in Sails, "that's what he wants. Get your pen, lad."

"Yes, Tyee, I will write you a letter."

"That is good," Maquinna said; and he went out to tell his people.

I poured some berry-juice ink into a clam shell, tore a clean page from my journal—the old *Boston*'s account book—and picked up my quill pen to write.

"Tell 'em to put him in irons, lad."

"Leave it to me, Sails," I said firmly, even angrily.

"Don't you draw back now," he muttered fiercely, thrusting his large face before mine. "I'd kill you, lad, if you was to draw back now. I've stood by you; and now you stands by me, like a proper shipmate."

"Have no fear, Sails. I know my duty. I don't like doing it, that's all. And now, if you please, allow me to write the letter without interruptions."

I was amazed at my own coolness, in contrast to my shipmate's sudden discomposure. Of the two of us, he had always been the cool one in an emergency; but now he was all shaken. For the first time, he felt that he could not be sure of me; that I might deceive him. My heart was heavy at the thought. I dipped the quill pen in the berry juice, and wrote:

To the Captain.

Sir—the bearer of this note is the Indian Chief, Maquinna, who wishes to trade with you. He has asked me to speak well of him, and this to the best of my ability I would like to do. But his tribe massacred twenty-five of the *Boston*'s crew in March 1803, the two survivors being now on shore. There is still a considerable quantity of the ship's cargo here, which by rights should be returned to the owners.

When Maquinna comes aboard we hope you will hold him, putting in your deadlights, and keeping so good a watch over him that he cannot escape from you. By so doing, we hope to make our escape in a few hours.

John Jewitt (Blacksmith of the *Boston*)
and for: John Thompson (Sailmaker of the same ship)

I read it over to my shipmate in a low voice, pointing to each word as I read it, to allay his suspicions. Then I took it out to Maquinna. He was on the beach, sur-rounded by his people. They were trying to dissuade him from his purpose, but he waved them aside. The tempta-tion to renew trade with the white men was too strong.

A canoe was run into the water, and Maquinna stepped aboard with the letter, a bundle of sea-otter furs, and six of his men. He sat amidships, erect and dignified. All eyes were upon him, both from ship and shore.

The canoe skimmed out, a strong arrow's flight across the Cove, to the Boston brig. We saw him climb the rope ladder to the ship's deck.

22

"Tyee Maquinna Trusted You"

It's worked, lad!" cried my shipmate, as we watched the ship from the door of Maquinna's longhouse. "The trick's worked! By Harry, it's worked!"

But he had spoken too soon. A few minutes later, we saw that one of Maquinna's party had eluded capture. He dropped over the side of the ship to the canoe beneath, which he paddled furiously toward the shore. A musket shot rang out from the ship's deck, but the Indian sped on, frantically paddling the canoe single-handed.

Maquinna's people were all down on the beach. When they saw the returning canoe, consternation spread among them, and this turned into a frenzy as the canoe ran ashore and the Indian told his woeful tidings—that their Tyee was a prisoner on the white man's ship and his under-chiefs with him. The women wailed and tore their hair; the children cried pathetically; the men massed to-gether, and moved in silent menace toward us.

We stood, side by side, in the doorway of Maquinna's house. Sails had a brace of pistols primed. He pointed them at the approaching men, but still they came on, slowly, silently.

"Don't shoot, Sails," I hissed.

"Not till they attacks us, lad. I'm ready for 'em, that's all."

The men saw this, and halted. They were a dozen yards from us, formed up in a semicircle, closing us in. They were quite silent, and still. It was the women and children on the beach who wept and wailed, making ges-tures of supplication toward the vessel in the offing, and running into the sea till the water was up to their waists.

But the men were silent. In a moment, they would rush upon us; my shipmate's pistols would explode; one or two Indians would fall to the ground; and then they would kill us.

"Men of Nootka . . ." I called out suddenly, upon impulse; but my words released a chorus of angry shouts.

"You bad man. *Peshak. Peshak.*"

"You tell Captain bad of our Tyee."

"You sell our Tyee to white men."

"White men put our Tyee in chains, like slave."

"We kill you."

"Kill you; kill you."

"Stop! Lay off that talk!" bellowed my shipmate. It

was an order these men had often heard from him, and always obeyed. They obeyed it now, perhaps from habit. "If you kill us," he threatened them, "you'll see Maquinna hanging at the yardarm on yonder ship, before the sun is set."

They were silent again, and bewildered. And then I found myself speaking to them once more, slowly, separating my words. I knew that I must make no mistake about their understanding what we were telling them.

"If you kill us—the Captain will kill Tyee Maquinna," I said. "Mark well what I am telling you, men of Nootka." I could speak their language almost like a native now, and I saw that my words sank in. "If you harm us, you will never see Tyee Maquinna alive again. But if you spare us, I promise you Tyee Maquinna will be brought back to you, alive and unharmed."

"White men, bad men," one of them cried. The rest remained glum.

"Was Captain Cook a bad man?" I asked. "Some of you remember Captain Cook. All of you have heard of him. Was Captain Cook a bad man?"

I paused, and shook my head at them. "No. Captain Cook was good. So was Captain Vancouver. So was Captain Salter. So were all our crew. Yet you killed our shipmates; you stole our cargo; you burned our ship. *That* was bad."

"Let 'em have it, lad. Lay it on strong," muttered my shipmate, but I was not noticing him. My eyes were riveted on the Indians, and I was carried along by a flood of emotion that was welling up in me, so that my voice shook, and tears fell from my eyes.

"I speak to you, not as the white lad whose shipmates were massacred," I continued, "but as one who has lived among you for many moons, making harpoons for your whale hunters, daggers for your warriors, and bracelets for your women. Listen, men of Nootka: I will go aboard the ship; I will tell the ship's Captain that you have spared me, housed me, fed me, treated me kindly, made friends with me. I will tell him all this, and more besides; and he will set your Tyee free."

I stopped, for I was out of breath, having raised my voice so that all could hear me. Sails was stunned into silence by my flow of words. But now the man who had previously spoken spoke again.

"How can we tell you speak true?" he said. "You spoke bad of our Tyee to the white Captain. You played him false."

Others were now echoing his words. "Tyee Maquinna trusted you, but you played him false."

I raised my voice above their cries. "Listen to me, men of Nootka. If you cannot trust me, listen to what you must do. Take me in Tyee Maquinna's canoe. Take me halfway out to the ship. Wait with me in the canoe out there, halfway between ship and shore. Keep me there till Tyee Maquinna is brought off the ship. We will change places. I will go aboard the ship. Tyee Maquinna will come back to you. Tom-soon will go out to the ship to tell the Captain what we are going to do."

The Indians turned to each other to discuss my plan. It seemed to appeal to them; and they seemed to be agreeing upon it. They moved toward the beach and the canoes. It was my shipmate who raised his voice at me in protest.

"Do I understand you to say I'm going out there first —before you? Well, I'm not. That's no part of our plan. I'm not going without you, lad. We go together, the two of us, or we stay together here."

"But you *must* go, Sails; to explain to the Captain."

"Explain what to the Captain? Tell him I've left you in the lurch; that I'm saving my own skin? Never!"

"You must go—to tell the Captain that they'll paddle me out halfway to the ship, where I'll change boats with Maquinna. Can't you see, Sails—it's the only chance left to us now. Look—they've got a canoe in the water; they're waiting for you."

A few Indians had indeed pushed a canoe into the water, and were holding it there. The rest, along with the women and children, had now joined the men outside the house. I saw the girl who had nursed me in my illness. Her head was lowered, and I thought she was weeping. Sat-sat, with a confused look upon his face, was striding up to me. But all my attention was on my shipmate.

"I don't like it, lad," he was saying. "I don't want to leave you. Sink or swim together, that's what we said."

"Please go, Sails. I tell you, it's our only chance."

Poor old Sails! He had fought so many battles, and now he was fighting one with himself. At length, he gave me one of his pistols and put a hand on my shoulder. He shook his head confusedly, went for his sea chest, hoisted it upon his shoulder, and walked away. His dog followed him, tail between legs. The Indians drew aside and made way for him; and he upbraided them, all the way to the beach. He swept his free arm from one side to the other with every admonishment.

When he arrived at the beach, he stepped into the canoe and dumped his sea chest amidships. His dog, following him aboard, jumped upon the sea chest, and sat there. Then the Indians took him swiftly out.

The whole village had flocked to the beach to watch his departure. I was glad to be relieved of their attention; but, at the same time, a great sense of loneliness settled on me.

I went indoors and sat on my bed, burying my head in my hands, for it was throbbing. The scar which remained from my wound on the day of the massacre burned under my fingers. I felt both dazed and baffled.

And Sat-sat-sok-sis stood before me.

23

Farewell to Sat-sat-sok-sis

"Tell me true. White men kill my father, John?"

These words of Sat-sat filled me with an instant pity. Here was this Indian boy, now on the verge of manhood, who, from the first day of my captivity had remained staunch to me. Always, he had been my steadfast and trusty friend. On several occasions I had owed my life to him. And now—how had I repaid him? I had betrayed his father, who was now in irons and at the mercy of the white men.

"White men kill my father. This I know. White Captain kill him." He raised his voice. "I will avenge my father," he said.

With a shock, it flashed through my mind that this boy was an Indian, and the customs of his people might prompt him to take revenge upon me now. But he had no dagger. And I reflected that I myself had had a share in this boy's upbringing.

"Listen to me, Sat-sat," I said. "I tell you, your father will come back."

"No. He will die."

"I promise you, he will come back," I said fervently, meaning every word. "He will come back, I say. And now, Sat-sat, your people are going to take me across the water. They are impatient to be going. So I must say good-bye."

"John not come back?"

"No." I slowly shook my head.

He seemed unable to comprehend. "Not—come—back," he murmured.

"Soon you will be a man, Sat-sat. You will take your father's place in the whaling canoe; and you will harpoon many whales. One day, you will become a great Chief. You will be friendly with the white men, and trade with them. So, now we will shake hands as the white men do."

"Yes, John."

"Good-bye, Sat-sat. Good-bye."

I turned to leave the house, and to make my way toward the beach. Inside my pocket was the pistol that Sails had given to me. I hoped with all my heart there would be no need to use it. I had become resigned to leaving my sea chest behind; and yet, when the time came, I could not bring myself to relinquish it. For one thing, my journal was inside, with a record of all that had

167

happened to us and to our ship from that fateful day in March, two years back. The Captain's writing desk I would have to abandon. Yet this grieved me, for the ship's papers were locked up inside it. Why had I not thought to transfer them to my sea chest! It was now too late to do so, for I could hear the Indians approaching the house again. With Sat-sat's help, I hoisted the sea chest to my shoulder, and left the house.

Outside, the people were returning from the beach. They had watched my shipmate go aboard the ship. They were in a state of great agitation and alarm. As I emerged from the gloom of Maquinna's longhouse into the bright light of day, I was greeted with angry cries.

I walked onward, looking neither to right nor left but straight ahead until I reached the shore. Two men had the canoe in readiness. It was only after I had waded out to the canoe, and placed my sea chest securely amidships that I saw Sat-sat, standing forlornly at the water's edge. He had silently followed me down to the beach.

"Good-bye, Sat-sat," I said again, "good-bye."

"You come back, John, one day," he said.

It was with a full heart and a confused mind that I placed myself in the bow of the canoe. My back was to the ship, and my eyes looked over the two paddling Indians to the crowded beach. I was alert for any hint of treachery. The women ran to Sat-sat and renewed their wailing, which carried alarmingly over the water.

We darted quickly out, skimming the water; halfway over, according to the plan, the Indians rested on their paddles, watching me steadily but uttering no sound. Now I could hear distant voices behind me, from the ship's deck. For a second, I turned my head to look. And in that quick glance, I saw the Captain with spyglass and speaking trumpet, and Sails standing beside him; and all along the deck, the crew were standing, their eyes fixed on our canoe.

They were waving me on, urging me to continue to the ship, and this created in me a sudden feeling of unease —of consternation: a mixture of alarm and doubt.

I knew what I was in honor bound to do. I had struck a bargain with the Indians on shore. I had promised to stop, halfway out.

The cries of encouragement from the ship continued, and indeed increased. At the same time, at the back of my mind, a nagging doubt persisted: the *Boston*'s papers were still ashore; much of the *Boston*'s cargo too—blankets, bales of cloth, chests of firearms, one or two barrels of gunpowder, and all those muskets and fowling pieces distributed throughout the village, which I had kept oiled and clean; and the only sure way to recover all these was to hold Maquinna prisoner until every item was brought safely aboard.

I do not excuse my action. I seek only to explain it. I had lived with the Indians for more than two years, observing how lightly they resorted to treachery; and I suppose I had learned a little of this myself.

The two Indians, resting their paddles, allowing the canoe to drift, regarded me steadily . . . suspiciously.

. . . I sprang to my feet, rocking the canoe. Taken off their guard, they lost their balance. One of them let go of his paddle, which slid from his hand into the water. The next moment, I had taken the pistol from my pocket and was pointing it at them. At the same time, I heard an outbreak of shouting, both behind me and in front. The shout from the ship was a cheer of approval and encouragement. But the shout from the shore was of a different order—for cries of baffled rage and anger rolled across the water in a wave of fury.

"Take me on," I shouted at the two Indians, in a sudden frenzy. "Take me on to the ship."

With a cry of fear, the Indian who had lost his paddle followed it overboard. I could see him swimming under the clear water, making for the shore. The remaining man, trembling with fear, paddled with all his might till we came alongside the ship—the good ship *Lydia*, a Boston brig. Soon, I had scrambled aboard; and with a welling up of emotion, impossible to describe, I faced the Captain.

24

The Long Trick's Over

In those first few moments on deck, I was taking everything in; the feel of the boards beneath my naked feet; the smell of hemp and tar; the curious questioning gaze of the seamen; the spars and rigging of this good ship, which reminded me in almost every detail of the *Boston*.

Sails came up to me, and clapped me hard on the shoulder. "Well done, lad!" He grinned. "I'm proud of you, son, and so is Jack here."

The dog jumped up and licked my face. Sails chuckled away to himself, turning his head in all directions, nodding and winking at the seamen around us, who nodded and smiled in return. They seemed unable to take their eyes off us, discussing together our outlandish clothing; and I could see more than one of them pointing out to a neighbor the scar on my forehead.

"Come into the cabin, Jewitt and Thompson," the

Captain was saying. "We've got this fellow Maquinna in irons and under guard."

The mention of Maquinna's name brought me back smartly to a guilty remembrance of what I had done to him. I entered the cabin with some foreboding. Sails, with a hand on my shoulder, followed me in, and closed the cabin door, shutting out the bustle and excitement of the deck.

There, in a corner, was Maquinna.

"*Wau-kash*, John," he said, forlornly.

"*Wau-kash*, Tyee," I replied, as I walked slowly toward him.

"What's the fellow saying?" demanded the Captain whose name, I learned later, was Hill.

"It's a form of greeting, sir; like saying *welcome*."

"The first word of their lingo we learned, Cap'n, on the day of the massacre," added Sails, with a wry grin.

"It *is*, is it! He deserves a sight warmer welcome than we've given him so far. What! What's this, Jewitt? Shaking hands with the rogue?"

"John, good," said Maquinna.

"And you're a scoundrel, sir," rapped out the Captain.

"No, Captain, by your leave," I said; "he's not, in all respects, a scoundrel."

The Captain raised his eyebrows in amazement. "I don't understand you, Jewitt," he said. "If he's not a scoundrel, then what is he? Something ten times worse? A murderer, for instance? Did he, or did he not take your ship and kill twenty-five of your men?"

172

"He did, sir. He and his tribe."

"And you make excuses for him? Come, Jewitt—have you lost your reason? Has your will weakened, lad? Have you lost all sense of right and wrong? Why do you seek to protect him?"

"He was provoked, sir."

"Provoked!" The Captain was baffled.

"In a manner of speaking, the lad's right, Cap'n," added Sails.

"Yes, sir, provoked," I went on. "By your leave, sir—in your eyes, and in mine, he committed a terrible crime. I won't deny it, sir. But he did *only* what all Indians do, according to their custom. He avenged a wrong done to his tribe."

"What talk is this? What wrong?" demanded the Captain, hotly.

"A wrong done by white men, sir," I answered, quietly; "by the Captain and crew of a trader, sir. They raided his village, stole his trading goods, and murdered some of his people."

"John tell true," said Maquinna, who was following the drift of our argument, and regarding me as his advocate.

"You hold your tongue, sir," rapped out the Captain. "I believe you understand more than is good for you."

"This harbor, sir," I went on, "is called Friendly Cove. Captain Cook put in here. He found the natives friendly. This chief, Maquinna, was a young man at the time. He was in his prime when Captain Meares, Captain Colnett,

Captain Dixon, and Captain Vancouver came again to Nootka. They were all here first with Captain Cook. Would they have come a second time, sir, each in the responsible office of Captain, if they had suspected Maquinna and his people to be treacherous? All these Captains spoke well of Maquinna. Unfortunately, sir, those who have come later have been less fair with the Indians. Some have been unscrupulous. Some have been callous. There have been killings and massacres on both sides."

The Captain turned to Sails who was nodding his head in agreement.

"Maquinna is no longer young, sir," I continued. "He has under-chiefs who give him trouble. But in his present plight I dare swear they would willingly die for him."

All the time that I was speaking, the anguished cries and wails of the Indians came over the water, to be heard by all of us on board. And the persistence of these cries began to tell on Captain Hill.

"You may be right, Jewitt," he said. "I daresay you may be right. But this man killed your friends—your own shipmates. Can you forgive him that?"

Sails stopped nodding, and began to shake his head instead. But I was not discouraged.

"*Yes, sir, I can,*" I said, after a moment's pause. "I am thinking mostly, sir, of Maquinna's son. He is a boy of twelve or thirteen, approaching manhood. He holds his father in great esteem; and Tyee Maquinna regards him with great affection. I have taught the boy our language. I have told him many stories about our people, of their industry and adventure. When he grows up, sir, and becomes a Chief, I am sure he will work for good understanding and fair trading with white men in these parts.

"If you hang Tyee Maquinna at the yardarm, sir, no white man will be safe along this coast. But if you set him free—"

"Set him *free!*" exclaimed the Captain, looking at me as though I were mad.

"I ask you to spare his life, sir; as he spared mine and Mr. Thompson's when others would have killed us. He has treated me with fairness; often with kindness. Have I your permission to remove the irons, sir?"

Captain Hill was completely baffled. He strode about the cabin, first one way, then the other; and all the time the muffled cries and the wailing of the Indians on shore reached us in the cabin. At last he stopped in his tracks.

"I don't know," he murmured; "I don't know." Then he faced me squarely. I noticed that his face was twitching strangely. "But why," he demanded, "why, in Heaven's name, if you want to set him free—why did you behave as you did in the canoe? Why the pistol?"

"Because, sir," I replied, "the *Boston*'s papers are still ashore, locked up in Captain Salter's writing desk; and in addition, there is still much of the ship's cargo in the village: muskets and fowling pieces; some bar iron and sheet copper; even a keg or two of powder still remains. I believe, sir, that Maquinna should be made to bring every remaining item of it aboard this ship before we put to sea."

"Yes, I see your point, Jewitt." The Captain turned to Maquinna. "Now, sir—" he began.

"My men bring," said Tyee Maquinna. "Muskets, blankets, all; my men bring aboard. I speak true."

The Captain looked contemptuously at him, then turned his gaze steadily on me. His eyes which were blue, were rather wide and staring.

"May I remove the irons, sir?" I begged him.

"Yes, Jewitt, you may," he said, without enthusiasm. "I hold you responsible for his good conduct."

Maquinna was looking at me with an expression half of gratitude and half reproach. I removed the irons; they had cut into his ankles. We went out upon the deck. All hands stood back, or moved silently away, with sidelong glances. The noise from the shore was unabated. At any moment, I feared, canoes would encircle the ship and close in on us, in a last desperate effort to save their chief. Maquinna looked sadly toward his village, but he was not without dignity.

"My people are afraid, John. My people are angry and afraid."

"Yes, Tyee. You must go back to them. The Captain has been merciful."

We shook hands; and as we did so, tears rolled down the Tyee's cheeks. It was a moment of strange melancholy, to be broken almost at once by the mirthful voice of Sails behind us.

"So Captin's set you free, Squire? Well—I reckon he's

right. Many's the time I've wanted to scalp you, Squire; but this lad wouldn't let me." He dropped his voice to a low, conspiratorial level. "Will you have a noggin o' rum to set you on your way, mate? Put heart into you, it will. You'll need it, mate, to face that rabble on shore. And then there'll be that Wic-an-an-ish lot turning up when you least expect it, and as full of tricks as a cage of monkeys. I'd have liked a go at that lot, I would. Will you have a taste of rum, now? *Cham-mas-sish*. Just say the word and I'll nick you some. You won't? Well, maybe you're right. I can see this son of mine scowling like thunder at his poor old dad." And saying this, he gave me a tremendous clap on the back, and burst into boisterous laughter which was taken up by seamen round about.

Maquinna descended into his canoe, and the five captive Indians were brought up from below to paddle him back to shore. At sight of this, the frenzy of the Indians on the beach knew no bounds. They leaped into the air, buried their faces in the sand, rolled over and over, and ran into the sea to meet their returning Chief.

"Just look at 'em," was my shipmate's comment. "Maquinna's welcome to 'em. You wouldn't drag me back to that Indian village, not for all the sea otters on the coast; nor for all the tea in China. Swabs they are—swabs and 'eathens." And he spat on the deck. He had not noticed Captain Hill standing behind him.

"Keep a civil tongue in your head and watch your behavior, my man," cut in the Captain sharply. "You will go easy with the rum, and you'll obey ship's discipline, or I'll have you put ashore again. And see to it that this dog is put ashore at once.

"Hold the canoe," he called out, over the ship's side. "Hold the canoe for this Indian cur to be taken off."

Poor old Sails! The dog whimpered a last good-bye and was lowered, struggling and showing the whites of his eyes, into Maquinna's canoe, which thereupon made for the shore with all speed.

The effect of the Captain's reprimand worked on Sails like magic. He shut up like a clam, and gave the Captain a wide berth till we were well out to sea.

Tyee Maquinna was as good as his word. Canoes came out with what remained of the *Boston*'s cargo; and more important, with the ship's papers, locked up in Captain Salter's writing desk. Load after load came aboard. It was surprising that so much remained. The cannon came aboard, and the ship's bell, and the lamps, and the spyglass, and the speaking trumpet, much the worse for wear. Cloth by the bale, blankets by the bundle, bar iron, copper kettles, and an incredible quantity of muskets came aboard. And finally the longboat was hoisted up.

During all this activity, I looked out for Sat-sat. It was my intention to seek the Captain's permission for him to come aboard and see over the ship. There was so much of interest I could have shown to him. But Sat-sat came nowhere near the ship during those last hours at Friendly Cove. Maquinna was taking no chances with his son.

When all was safely stowed away, and a little trade for

sea-otter pelts completed, we put out to sea. As we sailed out of the Cove and down the Sound, we saw upon the headland the tall figure of Maquinna, and by his side the figure of his son, with Jack, the Indian dog. And there they remained, outlined against the evening sky, till we were out of sight.

Some miles from Nootka, and sailing along the coast, Sails and I were still on deck, and looking toward the land. It was now dusk; but I could discern, faintly, a line of Indian canoes, under the shadow of the shore, moving in the direction of Nootka. I pointed them out to Sails. He screwed up his eyes in an effort to see them.

"They'll be that Wic-an-an-ish lot, I reckon," he observed, "on their way to plague Maquinna, as like as not. It'll come to war between those two. Ah, well; there's no peace for the wicked."

"No; I suppose not," I said, with a lump in my throat.

We filled up with furs along the coast, then made good passage across the Pacific, putting in first at Macao, then at Canton: then, finally, to Boston, Massachusetts.

Our voyage lasted a hundred and fourteen days. Little work was expected of Sails and myself, though we always turned to, and gave a hand with the working of the ship. I had plenty of time to write to my parents in Hull with the news of our rescue, and warning them that I rather thought of settling down in America.

At Boston, the owners were very kind to us. They helped us with gifts of money. With mine, I bought a smithy, and Sails joined me at the forge for a week or two. Then he decided to tie up his belongings in a bundle and take ship down the coast to Philadelphia, to the place where he was born.

So now I am on my own. Every day that passes, I miss my old, rough and rheumaticky shipmate. Neighbors call on me; and we talk, over the forge in my fine new smithy, about Nootka, and Maquinna the whale killer, and Sat-sat-sok-sis his son. The boys sometimes point to the scar on my forehead, and ask me how I came by it.

"Ah, that," I say, with a far-away look in my eyes, "that is a mark to remind me how I escaped scalping, in the massacre aboard the *Boston*, at Nootka, on March 22, 1803."

Author's Note

The history of the exploration of the Northwest Pacific Coast is an interesting story of adventure; but it is in some ways a sad story, a story of human greed and spoliation; a story of exploitation of primitive people. In 1741 Vitus Jonassen Bering explored the northern coast with Russian sailors. The ship was wrecked, and Bering died, but some of his men escaped in a boat, carrying sea-otter skins which they sold at a high price. This started a sea-otter fur trade with North China. The furs were landed at Okhotsk and taken overland to Kiakhta, the big fur market on the border of Mongolia.

Captain Cook, the great navigator, explored the coast in 1778, seeking for a northern passage from the Pacific to the Atlantic. It was the third of his famous voyages of discovery. He had on board several midshipmen who learned their navigation from him, and who later became famous captains in their own right: Captains Bligh and Vancouver, for instance.

It was in March, 1778, that Cook took *Resolution* and *Discovery* into Nootka Sound, and dropped anchor in a sheltered cove. He visited the Indians in their longhouses.

Cook's men traded with the Indians for sea-otter furs, which the chiefs wore as cloaks or mantles. The crew found them useful as bedclothes when they sailed north-ward through colder seas to the coast of Alaska. Eventually they sailed south to Hawaii, where Cook was so tragically killed by the natives; and by the end of 1779 they had reached Canton in South China. At Canton, to their surprise and delight, the men found—as Bering's men had found before them—that they could sell what remained of their much used and well worn sea-otter furs for very high prices.

This started up the British trade on the Northwest Coast. Ten years later, Captain Meares of the East India Company was pursuing the trade with ships called *Nootka* and *Sea Otter*. He made Nootka his base; and his Chinese carpenters built him a trading sloop which, when finished, was launched into the Sound and named *North-west America*. She was the first ship ever to be built on the Northwest Coast.

Besides Meares, at Nootka there arrived ships out of London, England; ships out of Boston; traders flying the flags of Britain, France, Portugal, Russia and America; and then, on May 5, 1789, two Spanish warships arrived on the scene and seized Nootka in the name of Spain.

The history books refer to this as "the Nootka Sound Incident." It nearly started a war between Britain and Spain. But Captain George Vancouver was sent with the *Discovery* to settle the matter in a peaceful and friendly manner on the spot. He arrived at Nootka in the summer of 1792. The Indian Chief Maquinna was there; so was the Spanish Commander, Señor Don Juan Francisco de la Bodega y Quadra. The three of them exchanged courtesies, and dined together. Vancouver and Quadra became good friends. They combined in a voyage of exploration, sailing round what proved to be a very large island, three hundred miles long, which they agreed to name "Quadra and Vancouver's Island." After fifty years this became shortened to Vancouver Island, as we now know it.

At Nootka the fur trade was now pursued mainly by American ships, from Boston, Massachusetts. The brig *Boston* under Captain Salter was one of these. The brig *Lydia* which rescued the two "castaways" was another.

The unfortunate sea otter became almost extinct, during a shameful period of cruel and unremitting slaughter. Since 1910, however, the sea otter of the Northwest Pacific Coast has been protected by law.

Some later nineteenth-century travelers, such as Robert Brown and C. M. Sproat (*Scenes and Studies of Savage Life*, 1868) have described Nootka as they saw it, and the Indians to whom they spoke. Some of the older Indians claimed to have remembered Jewitt and Thompson, or to have been told about them by their parents. Jewitt they described as a tall boy with a sense of fun, who sang and recited to them around the hearthfires.

The most vivid descriptions are to to be found among first hand accounts, in the large volumes containing the *Voyages* of Cook and Meares and Vancouver. A modern book with much interesting information is *Indians of the Pacific Northwest* by Ruth Underhill (published by the United States Department of the Interior, Washington, D.C., in 1945).

Michael Hyde was born in Oxfordshire, England, in 1908, and was educated in the Cotswolds and in Yorkshire. Before the Second World War, he taught in various schools in Hull. He served in North Africa and Italy during the war, and then returned to teaching, this time as Deputy Head of Cottingham Boys' School. In 1964 to 1965 he spent a year doing exchange teaching in New York State. He is now retired.

Mr. Hyde is married, with one daughter and two grandchildren, and his home is in Cottingham, Yorkshire. He is the author of *Arctic Whaling Adventures*, published by Oxford University Press, Inc., and has written radio scripts, and also verse and short stories which have been read over the radio.